'Chris, is a

'Joy, sit on [...]
something m[...]
Remember, you can leave at any time.' He
took a deep breath, aware of her puzzled eyes
looking at him.

'I didn't come here to leave.'

'You don't know what I'm going to say.' He
folded his arms, an unconscious gesture
showing unexpected rejection. 'Joy, I can't
marry you.'

'No one asked you to!' she said indignantly.
'Chris, that wasn't a proposal, it was just
that...I was wondering...' Then she started to
think about his words, scrambled to get off his
bed. 'You're married! That's it, you're
married! Right, I'm off now!'

Chris caught her, eased her back onto the bed.
'No, nothing like that. I'm not, never have
been married. There's no woman waiting for
me anywhere. This is something quite
different.'

Gill Sanderson is a psychologist who finds time to write only by staying up late at night. Weekends are filled by hobbies of gardening, running and mountain-walking. Story ideas come from work, from one son who is an oncologist, one son who is a nurse and a daughter who is a trainee midwife. Gill first wrote articles for learned journals and chapters for a textbook.

Recent titles by the same author:

A FULL RECOVERY
THE NURSE'S DILEMMA
LIFTING SUSPICION

MALE
MIDWIFE

BY
GILL SANDERSON

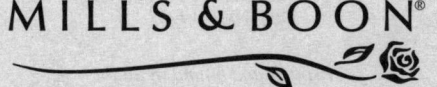

*All the characters in this book have no existence outside the imagination
of the author, and have no relation whatsoever to anyone bearing the
same name or names. They are not even distantly inspired by any
individual known or unknown to the author, and all the incidents are
pure invention.*

*First published in Great Britain 2001
Harlequin Mills & Boon Limited,
Eton House, 18-24 Paradise Road, Richmond, Surrey TW9 1SR*

© Gill Sanderson 2001

ISBN 0 263 82695 3

*Set in Times Roman 10½ on 12 pt.
03-1001-49913*

*Printed and bound in Spain
by Litografía Rosés, S.A., Barcelona*

CHAPTER ONE

CHRIS MCALPINE stood, a tall, white-clad figure in the door of number three low-dependency room, his face expressionless. In the room he could see Henry Trust, the obstetrics and gynaecology senior house officer, looking down at the panting woman on the delivery bed.

'Everything seems to be all right so far, Mrs Price,' Henry said indifferently. 'There'll be another midwife along in a minute. Sorry, but this one's a man.'

'You're a man, aren't you?' Mrs Price gasped. 'I don't mind what he is so long as he can help me.'

'Well, of course, but I am a doctor,' said Henry. 'There is a difference.'

Chris coughed and entered the room. He didn't want Henry to think he'd overheard. What Henry Trust thought or said no longer bothered him—the man was a mediocre doctor and a poor handler of people. But Chris had to work with him, so it was in the interests of their patients that they kept communications open.

Henry looked startled as Chris came in. He mumbled something about perhaps seeing him later and left promptly. Chris wasn't interested, he had a patient to see to.

'Hi, Mrs Price, I'm Chris McAlpine. Call me Chris. D'you mind if I call you Emma?' He beamed down at the straining figure below him.

'Call me what you like,' she said, 'just so long as we can get on with this.'

'Be right with you, Emma.'

He turned to the male figure standing uncertainly by the wall, offered his hand to shake. 'Joe Price, isn't it? I know this is a tough time for the husband as well as the wife, but I'm here to help you both through this. And everything seems to be going well, Joe.'

Chris always made a point of knowing the first names of his patient and her partner before he entered the delivery room.

'It's taking a long time,' said Joe. 'I didn't think it would be…like this.'

Chris knew this was Emma's and Joe's first baby. Even after films, discussions, all the attendance at the antenatal clinic, the actual physical details sometimes came as a shock.

'It'll soon be over,' he said reassuringly. 'Now, I'll just check Emma and then we can have a chat if you like.'

He turned to Emma, snapped on a pair of rubber gloves. At handover he had received the early labour record and had been told that Emma Price was having regular contractions and was already on the monitor. He still checked everything himself, then glanced at the clock on the wall. 'Half ten at night, Emma. D'you think you'll have this baby today or tomorrow?'

'Today would be best. I'm getting tired…ooh! That one hurt.'

Chris passed Emma the mouthpiece of the Entonox, the gas and air pain-relieving mixture. 'Take a breath of this. It'll make things easier.'

Emma did as she was told, and her tense body relaxed. 'Should we have the doctor back?' an anxious voice said from behind him. 'I don't want her suffering more than is necessary. What about one of those…epidurals, are they called?'

'I don't think it's necessary quite yet, Joe,' he said. 'But if it is, don't worry, I'll call.' Then something about Joe's voice made him turn. The man's face was pale and showed the sheen of sweat. 'It's very warm in here,' Chris said. 'Why don't you go for a walk down the corridor, perhaps get a breath of fresh air? Nothing's going to happen for a while and you'll feel better.'

'Yes, you go for a walk, Joe,' came Emma's voice, 'then you can come back and hold my hand.'

Joe thought a minute and then nodded and left.

'He's always been a bit queasy,' Emma whispered to Chris. 'But really he's excited and he's looking forward to the baby as much as I am.' She thought for a moment, and then said, 'Well, not quite as much. Ooh!'

'You're both doing fine,' said Chris.

Things progressed, though perhaps not quite as quickly as Emma wanted. Joe came back looking distinctly better and held her hand. He seemed calmer now. Chris knew that some couples needed to be constantly reminded of the midwife's presence, they felt lost without him. But now that Emma and Joe seemed quite self-contained, Chris would keep in the background for a while.

It was well past midnight and for a while Emma seemed to be tiring. Chris glanced quickly at the monitor. The baby was still doing well. Then suddenly Emma rallied. 'I've just got to push,' she said. 'I can't help it.'

Chris made a quick examination of the cervix. 'You're nearly fully dilated,' he said. 'Not long now, but pant instead of pushing.' He smiled encouragingly. 'You can do it.' Then he rang for assistance. There were always at least two present for delivery.

* * *

Tricia Patton, a trainee midwife, answered his call. Chris hadn't worked with her before but knew she had been with the unit for a month now—longer than he had. She was a tall, pleasant girl, at twenty-five or -six perhaps a bit older than many of the other assistants. Chris was pleased to see how she came and introduced herself to the parents-to-be—he knew it calmed people.

Now it was time for Emma to push. Chris could tell that the effort was tiring her but, red-faced and desperate, she did just what he told her.

'You're doing fine, Emma,' he said. 'Come on, not long now, you're going to have a baby!'

His enthusiasm was contagious. He caught Tricia smiling at him, and managed to wink at her.

But this baby just wouldn't be born. And it was so close. Chris decided to perform an episiotomy. He motioned Tricia to go to Emma's head, to talk to her loudly as he administered a local anaesthetic and made a short cut in the perineum. He knew Emma shouldn't feel any pain, but quite often the sound of the scissors' snip upset the patient. Then, at Chris's suggestion, Tricia got a mirror and showed the tired mum the baby's head emerging.

'Joe, our baby! I can see its head!' Emma's cry was one of half pain, half excitement. Then baby Price was born. First the head crowned. Quickly, Chris checked that the cord wasn't round the neck. Then, as Emma panted, one shoulder and then the rest of the tiny body slithered out. Chris let Tricia take the baby, quickly wrap her and place her for a moment between her mother's breasts.

Then he and Tricia stood back and waved Joe over so he, too, could see his new child. Chris noticed the silver of tears in the corners of the new father's eyes.

It wasn't an unusual reaction in the fathers of first-born babies—or, indeed, of others.

'I love this bit,' Chris said. 'It feels like a good job well done.'

He and Tricia let mother, child and father have a couple of minutes together, then they asked Joe to stand back so they could finish the rest of the processes to ensure that all was and would be well. The baby had to be assessed on the Apgar scale—given an assessment of heart rate, breathing, skin colour, muscle tone and reflex response. Three bands naming and identifying her were snapped onto her tiny limbs. This also was the time to stitch the perineum.

Just at this moment Henry Trust decided to drop in. 'Everything all right, Midwife?' he asked Chris.

'Chris here has been marvellous,' Emma snapped. 'He's made it all so easy for me. This hospital is lucky to have him.'

This didn't seem to be the news that Henry wanted to hear. 'Well, call me if necessary,' he said, and walked out again.

'He didn't even ask to look at the baby,' Joe said, amazed at the fact that anyone could not want to see his new child.

'Well, he's a very busy man,' lied Chris. 'Now, you're all finished here, Emma. I'll arrange for you to be taken to the postnatal ward. They've been expecting you and baby for a while. Isn't she gorgeous?'

'I've worked with other midwives, but they don't seem to feel it as much as you,' Tricia said. 'You were really, well, enjoying yourself there weren't you? It meant a lot to you.'

'Not as much as it meant to Emma and Joe,' Chris

said. 'But I think being a midwife is more than a job. It's a privilege.'

Tricia thought for a minute. 'I suppose it is,' she said, 'but you're the first person who has said that to me.'

'How d'you know when to perform an episiotomy and when not to?' Tricia asked Chris as they walked down the corridor towards the midwives' station.

He thought carefully before answering. He regarded it as part of his job to pass on what knowledge he could. While he'd been training there had been too many mid-wives who'd thought that students learned just by ob-serving. They had seemed to be unwilling to share their hard-earned knowledge. Chris believed this was wrong.

'You perform an episiotomy to avoid a tear in the perineum,' he said. 'I know you know that. A clean cut is easier to suture than a tear. If you see the skin thin-ning so much when the baby's head is pushing against it that you think it might tear, then you must cut. You saw that Emma's skin was stretched, white, there was no elasticity left in it. And the baby had been waiting to be born a little too long—a few more minutes and she might have been in distress. The next birth you help with, ask if you can look at the perineum and try to contrast the skin there with what you've just seen. I'm afraid experience is the only way of learning.'

'I see,' said Tricia.

They reached the midwives' station and both glanced at the whiteboard that held details of who was working where. Chris marked up the fact that Emma Price and baby had been sent to the postnatal ward and were no longer their responsibility.

'So you're enjoying working as a midwife?' Chris asked. 'It's just that some people are fine when they do the theory at college—but when they see the real thing, they aren't so sure.'

Tricia smiled. 'I've enjoyed every minute here,' she said. 'This is what I want to do. Before this I worked in a shop and it was terrible. Now, can I fetch you a coffee while you're writing up your notes?'

'Please. Strong, black, no sugar.'

He knew that note-keeping was a pain but had to be done at once, so he finished his report and then sipped the coffee Tricia had brought. It was just as he liked it.

At present neither of them were needed—babies came into the world unpredictably, and there were none on the way right now. So they had time to chat. On the other side of the room a midwife curled up in her chair and dozed, trying to catch a couple of minutes rest.

'Someone said you've not been here very long,' Tricia said cautiously. 'Just a couple of weeks or so.'

'That's right. I trained and worked in London before.'

'Are you—have you a wife up here?' With a rush Tricia went on, 'I asked because you're not wearing a ring, but if you have a wife, then perhaps both of you would like to come to the hospital barbecue. It's a week next Saturday, in Dennis Park.'

'I'm not married, Tricia, never have been, and at the moment no prospect of being. I saw a poster about the barbecue, it looked interesting.'

Trying to be nonchalant, Tricia went on, 'Well, there's a group going from the unit here. Perhaps you'd like to go with me, then? We could meet up with them.'

'Sounds like a good idea. But I gather Dennis Park's on the outskirts of town, and I won't want to drink much, so why don't you find another three or four pals and I'll drive all of you? I've got a biggish four-wheeler.'

Tricia was disappointed, but tried to hide it. 'That'll be great,' she said. 'I'll ask around.'

Chris finished his coffee and his notes, stood and stretched. 'Think I'll go for a stroll,' he said. 'I need to stretch a bit.'

'D'you find that working nights gets you down after a while?' Tricia asked.

'Not really, you get used to it.' But his face darkened as he thought about it. In his past he had often had to work nights. It wasn't something he liked to think about now. Still…midwifery was different.

The O and G unit was part of the hospital but self contained. Chris walked along the corridor and passed the other sections, the other wards. He moved silently but quickly. A careful observer might have noticed that he seemed to favour his right leg—there was a very slight limp. But it was almost imperceptible.

After the delivery suite there were the high-and low-dependency postnatal wards. He glanced through the doors, heard the sounds that now meant so much to him—the whispered conversations, the tiny cries of newborn babies. He smiled to himself. He was happy here.

He let himself out of the locked doors of the maternity unit and breathed the fresh air deeply. This was better than London! There was a warm wind from the Yorkshire moors behind him, but he fancied he could also smell the tang of salt from the sea. Yes, he was definitely happy here.

There was a little group of nurses and technicians clustered by a seat on the other side of the path, the glow of cigarette ends telling him what they were doing. No smoking anywhere inside Ransome General Hospital. You had to go out into the grounds. Chris smiled to himself and raised a friendly hand to a couple he recognised. He was glad he didn't smoke.

For perhaps ten minutes he walked hard across the lawn, passing the car parks and crossing the front of the A and E Department. Then he turned and walked equally quickly back. He would be bleeped if he was needed urgently, but he still didn't like being away too long from his post. He tapped in the code on the locked door and let himself back in. 'Anything doing?' he asked the two dozing staff in the midwives' station. Nothing was doing. He went to his locker, took out a textbook to read.

The rest of the shift was quiet. He was called at half past two to help with a birth, just as Tricia had helped him earlier. Then, at five a.m., a taxi arrived, carrying a calm Melanie Coutts and her husband. Melanie had three children already, and knew the drill. 'Contractions just over fifteen minutes apart,' she reported to Chris laconically. 'I knew I wouldn't get a full night's sleep tonight.'

Tricia helped Melanie get undressed and into bed, and then Chris came and booked her in. Her heart and blood pressure were recorded, the electronic monitor set up to check the baby's heartbeat. Chris gave his patient a quick internal, and found the cervix decidedly dilated. By the time he had finished the end of his shift was near. He left a settled Melanie, wished her good luck and went to hand over to Norma Parr, the midwife who would take over from him.

'Still enjoying it here?' Norma asked cheerfully. 'Still happy in your work? You know the first ten years are the worst?' She was an older woman, but Chris had worked with her and knew she was a conscientious and able worker.

'Still enjoying it,' he said.

Norma laughed. 'And you can't even get pregnant like the rest of us and have a few months off.'

'You never know what modern science might develop,' Chris said. 'Morning, Norma, I'm off.'

Just before he did leave he checked his pigeonhole, and found a note for him.

Dear Mr McAlpine,

Since you joined our unit while I was away, I would like to meet you and introduce myself.

I understand you now have a break of two days. As soon as you return could you arrange to see me as quickly as possible, please?

J. Taylor, O and G Nursing Manager.

It was a curt note, he thought. There was no word of welcome or congratulation on getting the post. Perhaps the woman was like that—although he thought the rest of the midwifery staff seemed to respect her. He knew the letter came from Joy Taylor, who had unfortunately been away on a course when he'd been appointed. She had neither seen him nor interviewed him. Chris shrugged. Now they would meet soon enough.

He walked out into a glorious early August morning, the air like champagne. It was too good to go to bed at once. He trotted down to the car park, jumped into his rather battered four-wheel-drive vehicle and drove the four miles home.

Home now was a tiny end-of-terrace cottage in a nearby village. He had leased the house for a year, and been given the option to buy it at the end of that time if he wished. There was a tiny front garden and a much longer back garden which had a glorious view over hills down to the sea. He knew nothing about gardening, he would have to learn.

He changed into his running kit and then ran easily down the little dead-end road that led to the clifftops. He never tired of this route. Sometimes he ran along it, sometimes he walked it, it was never the same. Below he could hear and see the sea, its salt scent in his nostrils. This could only be England and he was contented.

After half an hour he ran back, showered and made himself the lightest of breakfasts. As he ate he looked proudly round his little home. It was furnished sparsely—he wondered how many men of his age had so few possessions.

Finally he was ready for bed. His curtains were thick, he wouldn't be disturbed. For a while he stared at the ceiling, wondering if he would dream. He hadn't for a while. Then he was quickly asleep.

It was still fine when he drove back to work two days later. For a while he would be on earlies—working seven-fifteen in the morning till three in the afternoon. As ever, he arrived early—he liked to get his day well organised. He checked the rota and found he was working in the delivery suite again, although he had been told that in time he might be assigned to work in one of the other departments.

'No babies for you straight away,' said Alice McKee, the shift leader. 'Just fill in as you're needed. I've been asked to send you along to see Joy at nine. You know where her office is?'

'I know,' said Chris, 'I'll be there on the dot.' He felt not apprehensive but curious. Any leader—and Joy Taylor was a leader—could be judged by their department. And Chris thought this was a good one.

'So you're going to see our Joy, are you?' asked a junior midwife some time later. 'Not a very good name for her, is it? She's not very joyful.'

'She's not?' Chris asked neutrally. 'I thought people here liked her.'

'Oh, we all do! She's certainly the best boss I've ever worked for. But she's a bit of a career-woman. Appears to think of nothing but the job. I don't think she has much of a sense of humour either. And she's supposed to be going out with that SHO—Henry Trust.'

'If she's going out with Henry Trust then she must have a sense of humour,' said Chris. He felt he owed no respect to Henry.

It was second nature before going into a superior's office to check his shoes, uniform, hair. He knew it wasn't necessary—but now it was him. A voice called for him to come in when he knocked. He stepped into the office and resisted the automatic impulse to salute. 'Midwife Chris McAlpine,' he said. 'You wanted to see me.'

The woman behind the desk stood, extended her hand. 'Mr McAlpine,' she said coolly, her eyes still on the papers on her desk. Chris took her hand.

Then she looked up and their eyes met. And Chris McAlpine's carefully organised world fell apart.

Suddenly his life was different. He had never met a woman like this before.

But what was different about her, what was so special? Well…quite a lot of things really. But they all added up to one thing—she moved him more than any woman had ever yet done.

Unaware of any ill manners, aware only of the shock she had given him, he stared at her. What was happening to him?

It was happening to her, too. He could read faces,

and hers was now transparent. He knew what she was
feeling as surely as if she had told him. She felt just as
he did. There was the involuntary expansion of the pupil
in those glorious dark grey eyes. There was the held
breath, the licking of suddenly dry lips. Each knew what
the other was feeling. But neither could say anything.

They seemed to stare at each other for what seemed
an eternity. Then she half recovered, shrugging her
shoulders as if heaving off a weight, taking her hand
from his. 'Please, sit down,' she said, indicating a chair
in front of her desk.

Chris waited till she sat and then sat himself, silently,
and watched her look among the papers on her desk,
finding one that he recognised as his application form.
Both of them needed time to think, to adjust. She looked
down at the form as he looked at her.

She was taller than average. She sat well behind her
desk, her shoulders back. The lines of her crisp uniform
couldn't hide the generous curves of her body. Her hair
was dark, long, he thought, but held tightly to her head
in a French plait. The tightness of her hair emphasised
the high cheek bones. Her eyebrows were thick, dark,
not plucked, which he liked. Now her eyes were down-
cast, but they were large and grey, dark grey.

High on her left cheek was a mole and he half remembered…what did he remember? Well, there was the
eighteenth-century custom of wearing beauty spots, but
that wasn't it. He half remembered… Why was his
mind wandering this way?

Her mouth was wide, her lips full, but as he looked
at her he saw them tighten. She frowned, something
wasn't pleasing her. Whatever Joy Taylor had just felt,
she wasn't going to give way to it. She was fighting
back. She looked up at him almost angrily, as if be-

trayed by her own emotions. Well, he felt just as at his own feelings. But he knew his own face would give nothing away.

Smartly, she slapped the papers down on the desk, and the small noise seemed to wake both of them from some kind of trance. 'I'm Joy Taylor, Manager of the O and G nursing section,' she said. 'I'm sorry we haven't met before but I've been away on a course in London.'

'"Management for Senior Nurses in Hospital",' he said softly. 'Run by Professor Miriam Gee.'

Joy looked confused. 'You know about the course?'

'I've read about it in the nursing press and I've read both of Professor Gee's books. I thought the books were interesting. Her arguments for a nurse-led rather than a doctor-led hospital are very persuasive. Was it a good course?'

'Yes, it was a very good course. She often suggested that we…' Then Joy appeared to catch herself, to remember the job in hand. She looked down, shuffled her papers. Her voice lost its enthusiasm, became terse.

'I see you were appointed three weeks ago, but managed to start work after just one week? That was unusually speedy.'

'The hospital was short-handed,' he said, 'and I had some holiday time owing from my last job.'

'It was very good of you,' she said coldly, 'to be so helpful to us.'

'I like moving quickly.'

'Speed is all very well, but not in the delivery suite, I trust?' her voice was still cold, the words not meant to amuse.

'Babies tend to set their own pace,' he said calmly.

Joy turned over the papers in front of her. Chris sus-

pected it was to find something to do with her hands—
obviously, she already knew what was in them.

'I see you trained in St Matilda's Hospital in London,
and then worked there for two years. You got an excellent reference, they were obviously very sorry to lose
you. Why did you move?'

He wondered if he should point out that he had already been interviewed and appointed once. But then
he realised that he quite wanted to explain himself to
this woman. He wanted to know her. And he wanted
her to know him.

'I needed to move out of the city. I wanted somewhere with fresher air, purer water. And I wanted to
live in a community. In London, everyone seemed to
be just passing through.' He paused a minute and then
said, 'But, of course, I did get lots of experience there.'

'I can imagine.' Joy's voice got even more hostile. 'I
see before training for midwifery you were in the army
for seven years. Invalided out? Are you fit enough to
be a midwife?'

'Yes,' he said flatly. 'I limp a little but I can still run
ten miles. But not with a forty-kilo rucksack on my
back.'

Now she looked at him directly, an expression of
distaste on her face. 'Quite frankly, Mr McAlpine, I
can't say I have much time for military training or the
military mind. Some of the ex-soldiers I've come across
in hospital have not been…ideal.'

'Mr Garner was a soldier,' he pointed out slyly.
David Garner was the O and G consultant in the hospital. Chris had known him some years previously.

She coloured slightly. 'Mr Garner and I work very
well together,' she said. 'And I'm sure…I will work
with you, too.' It was said grudgingly.

'If you find I'm doing something wrong, I hope you'll tell me. I'm always ready to learn.'

'I'm sure.' She turned the pages in front of her restlessly, then returned to the attack. 'Why midwifery, Mr McAlpine? Why not nursing—perhaps A and E? I would have thought that dealing with trauma would have suited an ex-soldier much better.'

His voice was flat. 'I've seen enough trauma. And…'

'Yes?' Joy had noticed his hesitation, she was a shrewd interviewer.

He gave a soft answer. 'Midwifery just seemed right for me.'

She was obviously not happy with this. 'Could you be more exact?' she asked.

'Midwifery deals with health, not sickness or injury. It's life-affirming, it's positive. I enjoy it.'

At first she looked a little shocked at this. Then she recovered and said, 'That sounds like a speech you've rehearsed for interviews.'

'Quite possibly. But it's still something that's absolutely true.'

'Hmm. I have to say that I'm not really sure that I approve of male midwives. I think it one area of medicine perhaps best kept for the female sex.'

'That's not an uncommon point of view. But I've found it held more often by older midwives than by the mums I've had to deal with.'

Joy persisted. 'My personal experience of male midwives has not been a good one. I've worked with two. One was just generally poor. The other thought he was God's gift to women and caused no end of trouble. However, you are entitled to be judged on your own merits.'

He wondered if the questioning would stop now. Joy

Taylor appeared to be driven by some inner force, he was still not sure why she had taken against him so much. Perhaps this was her way of coping with that sudden flash of attraction that they both had felt. He wasn't sure how he was going to cope with it himself.

'You know there was another applicant for this post?' She was returning to the attack. 'Paula Charles—she did some of her training here. I thought she was a good candidate and I gave her an excellent reference.'

'Yes, I met her. She wasn't too upset at not getting the job, she knows there'll be plenty of Bank work for her. Would you have preferred her?'

But Joy was not going to be drawn. 'The board's decision is final. I notice you got a really remarkable reference from Mr Garner, and very properly he removed himself from the voting because he said he knew you.'

'We were in the army together for a time,' Chris acknowledged.

'And so…?'

'And so I hope I prove worthy of his recommendation.'

Chris wasn't going to talk about his time in the army. However, he felt that he could offer something. 'I can understand your displeasure,' he said. 'You didn't get the person you wanted, you don't like the military mind, you don't like male midwives. All possibly legitimate grounds for complaint. If you can tell me honestly in six months that I'm not up to the job, then I'll leave.'

This shocked her. 'You mean that, don't you?' she asked after a pause.

'I don't say what I don't mean.'

'Well…' Suddenly Joy was confused. 'You've just joined my unit and I don't think I've ever been so unwelcoming to anyone… I'm sorry, I'm sure you'll do your job well here. Please, don't take any offence.'

'I shan't,' Chris said, 'I like plain speaking.' There was a pause and then he said, 'Should I go now?'

'Oh…er, yes, of course. And do remember that if you have any problem at all I'll be happy to discuss it with you.' She smiled unhappily, obviously aware that this little remark didn't fit in well with what she'd said before.

He stood, and then it came to him. He spoke before he could stop himself. 'Margaret Lockwood,' he said.

'I beg your pardon?'

'Sorry,' he said, now confused himself. 'Just something personal that I suddenly remembered.'

'Margaret Lockwood? You'll have to tell me, I'm intrigued.'

He sighed. He hadn't intended to get into this. 'You have a mole on your cheek and it reminded me of someone. I couldn't think who, and then it came back to me. Margaret Lockwood. She once played a highwayman— or -woman. She was very big in English films in the late nineteen forties, she was a famous beauty.'

'Oh,' Joy said, obviously at a loss. 'I think I've seen her. On TV. She's not at all like me. That'll be all, Mr McAlpine.'

'Thank you ma'am,' said Chris. 'And—please—call me Chris.'

Then it was just another day. Chris delivered a baby, assisted with two others. When he had time he dropped in on the postnatal ward to say hello to Emma Price and her new baby girl. He liked to do this at least once to show the new mums that they were more to him than just a job for a few hours

Once he passed Joy in the corridor, walking that quick nurse's walk. It pleased him to see how gracefully she moved, her body as beautiful in movement as it was in repose. He said, 'Good afternoon,' and she nodded, smiled tightly and returned his greetings. He wondered if the short exchange had meant as much to her as it had to him. He hoped it had.

Finally there was another baby to book in, then handover at three to the incoming midwife, and change and go home. An ordinary day—after his first meeting with Joy Taylor.

In his cottage Chris changed again, this time into his walking gear and then drove twenty miles to the top of the Yorkshire moors. For a couple of hours he walked, as he so often did, to exercise his body and clear his brain. Then he stopped, sat in a little corner formed by rocks, and looked down at the view. In the valley below there was a village and he could see people, tiny dots to him, but with their own lives, their own worries, their own concerns. He swigged from the bottle of water he carried, ate a digestive biscuit.

He was thirty-two. Most of the people he had been at school with were now settled, most of his friends married or in long-term relationships. But he wasn't. He liked women. He got on well with them, in spite of sometimes appearing a bit of a macho figure. During his seven years in the army he had never felt sufficiently attracted to any woman to try to form a permanent relationship. He had known several—had been fond of them—but by mutual consent nothing had come of them. Then he'd had to leave the army.

Training as a midwife and then practising as one had given him many chances of meeting attractive, available women. He had taken out more than a few—but had never yet met the woman he wanted to spend the rest of his life with.

So what about Joy Taylor? First of all, she didn't like him. Well, she didn't like the Chris McAlpine who had been presented to her by the application form. But there had been that sudden flash between them, that spark that both had recognised. Yes, both of them had recognised it. And both of them knew that the other had felt it. So both of them were vulnerable.

He just didn't know what to think or do. He had been told that Joy was a career-woman, but instinctively he knew just what she wanted. It was so ordinary and yet so precious. She wanted a home, a husband, children, probably a career fitting round them. A package he couldn't give her.

He had never expected this when he'd come to Ransome General Hospital. He had wanted fewer problems, not more. Perhaps he would leave in six months. But he didn't want to. He wanted to stay and see more of Joy. Something between them would have to be settled.

CHAPTER TWO

'I THINK I'd like to see you actually at work,' Joy said to him abruptly next day. 'I'm not checking up on you, but I like to see how all of my staff perform.'

It was early, just before the seven-fifteen handover, and she had come to find him in the midwives' station.

'I think that's a good idea,' Chris agreed. 'It's fine by me and you've got every right. But you know two of your shift leaders—Alice McKee and Alison Ramsey—have already been in to watch me?'

Joy coloured slightly. 'Yes, I do know. And both have reported very favourably on your work. But I still need to make up my own mind.'

'In that case, I'll phone your office when I'm assigned my next case.'

She turned to go, and then turned back again. 'Incidentally,' she said with an air of great indifference, 'I was in the library last night and I...came across a picture of Margaret Lockwood. She's not in the least like me.'

'Different hairstyle,' Chris agreed, 'though I don't know if you let it down. But you both have that mole and you both are very attractive women.'

He knew he shouldn't have said it. He knew it was unprofessional. But there were times when you just had to take a risk.

Perhaps it had paid off. She grew a little pinker and said, 'Well, phone me when you have a case in and I'll be along.' Then she walked away.

He watched her go. He had found just a little chink in her armour. Good.

'June Tilling,' said the midwife he was taking over from. 'She's just starting second stage. However, the head's quite high. The only trouble is that the husband's a bit awkward. He insisted on sending for the doctor once. I thought I'd let him get away with it to keep him quiet. But then Henry Trust came along and decided to be unhelpful, and so now the man is simmering with rage. An older couple, this is their first baby.'

'Great,' said Chris, thinking this was just not the case he wanted Joy to observe. 'Is the mother OK?'

'She's a darling. Very calm, very long-suffering—I guess she has to be with that man. Good luck, Chris, you'll need it.'

First he phoned Joy and then he walked to low-dependency room two. The minute he got inside he knew the kind of man the husband was going to be. He was peacock-erect, aggressive. 'Who're you?' he barked when Chris entered the room. 'What are you doing here?'

He was a small man, with a fancy waistcoat and a nasty moustache. He hadn't unbuttoned his collar, even thought he must have been very warm. Chris had met men like him before. He knew there would be no appealing to reason, no calm consideration. He also knew the man wasn't too interested in his wife, he was more interested in his role as a prospective father.

Well he, Chris *was* interested in the wife.

'I asked what you were doing here,' the man snapped again.

'I'm Chris McAlpine, your midwife.' He turned as the door opened behind him and saw a figure, now dressed like himself in uniform. 'And this is Miss Taylor, who is Manager of the O and G unit.'

'We'll have her. We don't need you, we don't want a man. We have rights, you know.'

'Of course you have, Mr Tilling. We will ensure that your rights are respected. Now, will you wait outside, please, while I examine your wife.'

'You're not going to do that!'

'I shall be here, Mr Tilling, and I can assure you that all will be well.' This was Joy, magnificently chilly.

Good, thought Chris, she's made the same assessment of Mr Tilling as I have. If we give way one half-inch to this man there'll be no end of trouble.

'Well, I'll be back in ten minutes. But I don't like it.' Mr Tilling stalked out.

Now Chris turned and introduced himself and Joy to their patient. As the previous midwife had said, Mrs Tilling was a darling.

'Don't pay any attention to Harold,' she said anxiously. 'He's bothered because this is our first baby and I'm an older mother.'

'You have no objection to having a male midwife have you?' asked Joy.

'No—Ooh. I think it's rather nice. But Harold does go on sometimes.'

'Right,' said Chris, 'now, if you can just relax, Mrs Tilling. D'you mind if I call you June?' Watched by Joy, he started on the series of tests—temperature, blood-pressure and pulse—that were taken regularly. He also glanced at the monitor and noted the foetal heart rate. In a moment he would write down all these observations, but first he had to get to know his patient better. As he worked through the necessary tasks he talked to June—about unimportant things perhaps, but enough to make her think that someone was interested, someone was paying attention to her.

'Mind if I feel your tummy now?' he asked with a smile.

'Yes, yes…whatever you need to do.' Carefully he palpated, then took the mother's hands and gently showed her where to feel. 'Now, feel this smooth bit? That's your baby's back. And here on the other side, these sticky-out bits are the arms and legs. And last of all—feel with two fingers of each hand—that's your baby's bottom.'

'It's big,' said June with a gratified smile. 'Can I feel the head?'

'No. The head is now firmly locked into position. Can't you feel it bashing away at you?'

'Ow,' said June. 'Yes, I certainly can.'

When he had finished his examination he said, 'I'm just going to have a word with Mr Tilling. Miss Taylor, if you will remain here.'

Joy looked at him dubiously. 'You think that's wise?'

'I see no reason why not. And I know Mr Garner is around here somewhere. I thought I might ask him just to drop in and look at Mrs Tilling. No need, of course, just for reassurance.'

'Whatever you think,' Joy said, looking surprised.

Chris found Mr Tilling drinking coffee and complaining loudly about it. He took the man aside for a quiet word. 'I understand your worries, Mr Tilling,' he said, 'but there is absolutely no need for them. We know Mrs Tilling is an older mother. May I say I'm a fully qualified, experienced midwife, and will do everything in my power to make sure things run smoothly. Incidentally, we're arranging for the consultant to see your wife—no need really, just a little extra courtesy on our part. But he's a man, too.'

'You're trying to trick me!'

'No, Mr Tilling, we're just trying to do our best for your wife and child. The entire hospital wants that. But if you're still dissatisfied and Mrs Tilling signs herself out, we can arrange for an ambulance to take her to a nursing home of your choice. Though I wouldn't recommend it.'

Chris's gamble paid off. Mr Tilling gave way and muttered, 'OK, you can stay. I'm…very happy with that.'

'I'm Chris by the way.' Chris beamed, extending a hand. 'And you're Harold?'

'Yes,' gulped Harold.

'We'd better get back, then.' Chris led the way to the room and announced to the two women inside, 'Harold and I have had a little talk, and he's happy for me to stay.' He saw Joy looking at him suspiciously, but he kept a bland face.

After that all was straightforward. He had seen his friend David Garner, the consultant. David dropped in for two minutes, conducted a lightning examination of June and said she was doing fine. Mr Tilling held tightly onto his wife's hand.

They were now well into stage three. The contractions were now one in three—one in every three minutes—and Chris knew the birth was imminent. 'You're enjoying this, aren't you, Chris?' June panted.

Chris checked the cervix again. 'Well, I'm not enjoying you having the pain,' he said, 'but look—or feel rather.' He took June's hand, ran it over her distended abdomen. 'That's your baby pushing.' He smiled at her as he let his hand rest next to hers. 'Isn't it magic? And you're going to be a mother soon. Something that only a woman can do, and honestly I envy you. There'll only be discomfort for a while longer, then you'll have your baby and you and Harold will be entranced at what you see. Then you'll feel more tired than you have ever in your life before. You'll be so happy, though. You'll sleep, but it'll be a good sleep. And then you'll wake and your life will never be the same again.'

Even through her pain June could be curious. 'You're an odd man,' she said. 'You seem to know more about what I'm feeling than both of the midwives I've seen already. And you seem to care about me even though we've only just met. How did you come to train as a midwife?'

He told her the truth—though perhaps not all of it. 'First of all, I do care for you. Being allowed to help you, being allowed to witness someone being born, is a privilege. After a day on the unit here I go home fulfilled. There's not a lot of men can say that about their job.'

'I think you're a lovely man, I—ow!'

'Have some more gas and air,' said Joy.

When it was time Chris smiled encouragingly at June. 'I can see your baby's head now—it's crowning. Not long now, everything's going fine. Now, when I tell you, push—but not until I tell you. June, this is great! You're doing really well!'

He told her to push on the next contraction, and as the baby's head started to emerge he carefully held it to prevent it coming out too fast. The whole head slowly came into view, he ran a finger under the chin, checked there was no cord obstruction. And as the anterior shoulder came further down the birth canal, the baby's head started to turn.

'All going well, June, you're doing a wonderful job. Now, don't push till I tell you!'

For some reason he looked up at Joy, who was regarding him with a perplexed expression. 'I love it when the baby just rolls round like this,' he said. 'I think Mother Nature has done a really clever job.'

'You're not having the baby,' Joy muttered, 'but I know what you mean.'

Then, with a great shriek of excitement from June, the baby was born. 'It's a little boy!' Chris announced. Joy took him, wrapped him in the prepared towel and placed him on his mother's abdomen. Just for a moment. But the bonding could start at once. Chris was glad Joy had done this—some midwives believed that the baby should be checked instantly, but he felt that if there were no causes for alarm, then mother and child should be together as quickly as possible.

For June and Harold the excitement was just starting, for the two midwives the rest was just procedure. Important procedure, of course. Chris took great pains to see that everything was done according to the book. But his job was now largely done. The important people were June, Harold and the baby.

Soon it was over. June was overjoyed with her little boy, and even Harold seemed moved. He shook Chris's hand fervently, apologising over and over again for his behaviour. Then mother and baby were dispatched to the postnatal ward, and Chris's work was done.

'Did I pass?' he asked Joy, tongue in cheek.

'You know very well you did. You're a competent and assured midwife. However…there are a couple of things I want to take up with you. Come to my room and we'll have a coffee.'

'Let me finish the paperwork,' Chris said, 'and I'll be right along.'

Joy's coffee was distinctly better than that available in plastic cups in the midwives' room. She served it as he liked it—hot, black, sugarless and strong. She even gave him a chocolate biscuit. 'There was something you wanted to ask—or tell me,' he said.

'Yes. As I said, your midwifery is fine. But how did you deal with the husband? I thought we might have trouble with him.'

Chris shrugged. 'You saw the kind of man he was. I offered him a little reassurance, told him the alternatives and he gave way. He only wanted to flex his muscles a bit.'

'He seemed a bit over-excited when we arrived— more than I would have thought.'

Chris looked thoughtful for a minute and then said, 'Perhaps he was upset by an earlier visitor?'

'What kind of earlier visitor?'

'Well, I gather Henry Trust was in the room.'

Joy reddened. 'Dr Trust is a very competent practitioner!'

'I am sure his medical qualifications are admirable,' said Chris. 'I'm not accusing the man, I'm just bringing something to your attention.'

He guessed that Joy didn't really want to talk about the matter. That was fair enough, but he had done what was necessary by suggesting something to her. If she were a good departmental leader, she'd make her own enquiries.

There was a short silence then Joy said, 'I've told you that you're a competent and assured midwife. But you're more than that. You were quite…moved by it all, weren't you?'

He felt uneasy. 'I hope all midwives feel that way,' he said.

'I'm sure they do. I do. And I recognised just a bit of what I feel in you. It…interested me.'

He decided he wanted to change the subject. 'Are you going to this barbecue in Dennis Park?' he asked. 'Apparently a lot of our staff are going.'

'I don't think so. It's not really my kind of thing. Er…are you going?'

'Tricia Patton told me about it. I offered to take her there.'

Joy frowned. 'I'm glad members of my staff are going together. Of course, you may go with whom you like—but I would have thought that Tricia was a bit young for you.'

Keeping a straight face, Chris said, 'I think it's a very good management policy to see and be seen at hospital social functions. It makes people work together better.'

'I hope you're not telling me how to manage my department! And I run a midwifery unit, not a platoon of soldiers.'

'I wouldn't dream of telling you how to manage. But, I must say, the army isn't all that different from a hospital. Incidentally, when I offered to take Tricia Patton I also said I'd like to take some of her friends. No way would I encourage her to think that there could be something between us.'

'No fraternisation between ranks?'

Chris grinned. 'Miss Taylor, that's a joke about a sacred subject. Thanks for the coffee, I'd better get back.'

It was still early afternoon when he got back to the midwives' station, and when she saw him Alice McKee bustled straight up to him. 'Chris, you can do us a big favour. But if you don't want to, or if you've got anything planned, just say so. I mean that.'

'What's the problem, Alice?' Chris liked the shift leader. She was calm, efficient. He'd help her if he could.

'We've got two midwives just phoned in sick from the night shift. Di Owen and another one. There's no one we can get from the bank. How would you like to go home right now, try to get some sleep in and come in for the night shift? We can give you an extra day off tomorrow, and pay you properly. I'm sorry to ask you this, but you know our staffing is right down.'

Chris did know. 'I'll do it,' he said. 'I'll always help out if I can.' In fact, it wasn't something he was looking forward to, but he knew Alice would only have asked him if it had been necessary.

'You're a darling.' Alice reached up and kissed his cheek. 'Now, you go home and try to get some sleep.'

So he went home, buying a book on gardening on the way. For a while he pottered out in the garden, and then came in and tried to get a few hours' broken sleep. All part of a midwife's job.

As always he was in promptly. Handover was quick. There was a birth imminent and he got to the room just in time for the delivery. It was straightforward, there was no husband, and just after midnight the mum and her new child were trolleyed to the postnatal ward.

Then there was little to do. There was another midwife in the staffroom, Janet Fell, with whom Chris had worked before. Janet was a small, round girl, now six months pregnant herself, and already booked in here at her own unit. 'I shall be watching you, making sure you get everything right when I come in,' she had told her friends. She was working as long as possible so she could have more time off afterwards.

'You go and find somewhere to sleep,' Chris told her, 'I'll look after things here.'

'I'll do no such thing,' Janet said sturdily. 'If I can't do the job I won't come in.' Chris liked this attitude.

But there was nothing for either of them to do.

After a while Janet said the close atmosphere was getting her down and she would walk over to the A and E Department to see a friend there. She carried her bleep, and if needed she could be back in five minutes. 'That's fine,' Chris said.

He read a couple of magazines, considered having a doze himself, then a third midwife came in. Her case was over, the mum sent off to Postnatal. And this midwife *was* going to doze. Chris said he, too, would go for a breath of fresh air, perhaps meet Janet.

The coolness of the night was calming after the heat of the delivery suite. He passed the little knot of smokers and set off across the grass towards A and E. He had to cross a dark patch of lawn, not illuminated either by the car-park lights or the hospital lights. There were mature trees growing here, and nurses sat under them in the day.

He wasn't sure why it happened. Perhaps years of being on patrol had given him a sixth sense. Perhaps, out of the corner of his eye, he saw branches waving where there was no breeze. Perhaps there was some sound, too low for conscious recognition. But first he froze. Then he slipped silently into the shadow of a tree.

A bit of his mind registered that he was in a bright white uniform. Ludicrous. He should be wearing camouflage and have a blackened face. He told himself he was imagining things but still he slid from tree to tree, old skills coming back to him.

Violence against hospital staff was a growing problem. He had got half-accustomed to it in London but he hadn't expected it here. But part of him sadly knew that it was now everywhere.

He peered round a tree trunk. On the other side of a little clearing was Janet, her back against a tree, a man holding her there with his hand across her mouth. In his other hand was a knife. He hadn't heard Chris sneak up.

Chris heard him whisper, 'I'll take that handbag and one sound out of you and I'll cut you.' But brave, stupid Janet was refusing to let go. Chris heard her try to call out.

The first thing to do was to get the man away from Janet so, abandoning all concealment, Chris walked loudly and boldly across the clearing. 'But will you cut me?' he asked.

The man turned, tearing the handbag from Janet's grasp. She slumped to the ground. Chris was glad she didn't scream, which might have unnerved the man, made him act unreasonably.

'We can sort this out quietly,' said Chris. 'No need for violence, I—'

The man leaped forward and lunged, the knife stabbing towards Chris's chest. Chris moved to one side but heard the ripping of his tunic, felt the numbness that often came with a cut. But then he was lucky. His own desperate punch connected firmly with the man's jaw. The man dropped, unconscious.

Chris hurried to Janet, stooped over her. 'How are you feeling? Did he hurt you at all?'

'Get my handbag back,' came the reply. 'I'm all right. Don't let that man get away with it.'

'I don't think he's going anywhere in a hurry,' said Chris. 'I think I've knocked him out.' But he picked up the handbag. Then he carefully turned the man over into the recovery position.

His first reaction was to pick Janet up and carry her to A and E. Then he thought better of it. He saw a couple he recognised walking to the car park, so he shouted to them to go to A and E and fetch two trolleys and a couple of nurses.

'Has there been an accident?' one of the two asked.

'You could say that,' said Chris.

'We've got a man on guard outside the ward,' said WPC Ralston, 'but I doubt he'll be needed. The doctor says that the mugger isn't likely to move for a day or two. That was certainly some punch!'

'I tried to talk to him,' said Chris, 'but Janet Fell is pregnant and I felt I had to—'

'You did just fine! Now, I don't like asking you this, but we have to be certain. You didn't use anything that could be described as an offensive weapon, did you? No stick or anything like that?'

'Nothing,' said Chris. 'In fact, I skinned my knuckles.'

'Good. It would have been all right, of course, especially since you were injured, but it does simplify things. We've recovered the knife, we're getting a statement from that poor midwife and we know the laddie in question. We've managed to do him a couple of times, but we think he's got away with a lot we don't know about. You've done the women of this town a favour. You're a nurse, you say?'

'I'm a midwife.'

'A midwife?' WPC Ralston's tough but rather attractive face broke into a smile. 'I've had one kid and we're thinking about another. If I book in here will you see to me? I'd feel safe with you.'

Chris grinned wearily. 'I'd like to. But you know, you have to take your chance.'

'We're going to need more statements, make more enquiries. In the end there'll be a court case. His brief will almost certainly tell this fellow to plead guilty. If so there'll be no need for anyone to appear. But if he pleads not guilty, how d'you feel about appearing in court?'

'I'm not very happy,' said Chris. 'The hospital could do without the publicity. But I believe absolutely that it's got to be done. I'll stand up in court if necessary.'

'I wish there were more like you,' said the WPC.

Fortunately, no more mums-to-be called in that night. Janet was admitted for the night, in spite of all her protests. The shift leader insisted on it. Her husband was brought in. It seemed to Chris that the entire hospital staff was wakened. He saw the head of security, the A and E consultant, a hurriedly summoned senior manager. All wanted to talk to him.

Eventually the A and E consultant shouted that it was three o'clock in the morning. He was taking charge and insisted that Chris go to get some rest. 'This man has had a very nasty cut, he's lost blood. I've dressed it and I think he should stay off work for a week, but he says there's no need. But no more questions!'

Chris said, 'The police know I was injured, but I'd be grateful if it could be kept quiet in the hospital. I don't want more fuss.'

The consultant nodded. 'Whatever you say,' he said.

Chris didn't want any more trouble so he undressed, swallowed the two painkillers he had been given and climbed into bed. He had accepted a bed in one of the little rooms that were kept for parents who needed to sleep near their children. His side was throbbing, but somehow he slept.

In the morning he woke up a hero. A ward sister brought him breakfast in bed, and said that everyone thought he was wonderful. About six months ago, she said, there had been a similar attack—perhaps by the same man—and a nurse had been badly punched in the face.

Chris got up and dressed. When he phoned down to A and E to ask after Janet, he was told that she was fine and had been sent home. 'It was either that or tie her down,' said the voice.

He was embarrassed when he got to the midwives' room. He had his back slapped, was kissed, congratulated. The shift leader said he was to go home. He refused. He'd had his sleep and wanted to work.

A voice snapped, 'He can work later. Chris, could I have a word please? In my room?'

It was Joy. And from her expression she wasn't very happy.

'The hospital doesn't want this kind of publicity, this kind of reputation,' Joy said coldly when he was sitting in her room. 'We wanted a midwife, not a…brawler. Of course we were glad you could help Janet—it's good that she's a tough little thing and it could have been so much worse. But I've talked to the A and E staff. You practically broke the man's jaw. Couldn't you have…just taken the knife off him?'

'I did try to talk to him. But he didn't seem in the mood for conversation.'

'This isn't funny, Chris!'

He wondered about her. She was angry, of course—he could even sympathise with that. Anger was a common way of dealing with shock. But there was something more. Talking to him like this was the only way she could cope with that instant attraction they had both felt. He felt it still. He thought she did, too. But would she ever own up to it? Accept it?

For a while he looked at her expressionlessly. Then he reached across and started to unbutton the new tunic he had put on that morning. 'What are you doing?' she asked, obviously shocked, but he didn't answer her.

Chris slipped off his tunic and pulled his short-sleeved shirt over his head. Now he was naked to the waist. He lifted his left arm, pointing to the strapping along his side. 'I'm afraid I wet the dressing when I showered this morning. It's only a scratch really, but—'

'You were hurt! I didn't know that.' Now Joy's voice quavered.

'I told you, I did try to talk to the man, but he still tried to stab me. With a seven-inch blade. I moved but not quite fast enough. Just tell me what would have happened if his aim had been four inches to the left.'

White-faced, she came round her desk, lifted his arm and looked at the strapping. She measured, with a shaking hand. 'It might have bounced off a rib,' she faltered, 'but most likely it would have gone straight into…the heart.' He saw her gulp at the words.

'It's all right,' he said gently. 'It didn't go into the heart. I'm alive.' Then he grinned. 'You won't be advertising for another midwife just yet.'

'I said it before, this just isn't funny! It's not funny at all!'

'Sorry. Just that sometimes the best way of dealing with trauma is laughing at it.'

'Not in my unit. Not for me. You could have been…' He saw her trying to get control of her feelings. Her fingers trembled as she touched the dressing. 'You're right. This is wet, it needs replacing.' Trying to be professional, she went on, 'I take it that you're up to date with your antitetanus jabs and so on?'

'Of course. But there's no need for you to do this. I can drop in at A and E and—'

'I was a nurse before I was a midwife. I can do it. Sit there while I fetch a dressing and stuff.'

So he sat in her room. He'd never been in there on his own before. It was a small room, without a single personal touch in it. Other, similar rooms he'd seen had had photographs, or a vase of flowers, or a few potted plants. Not this room. It was neat and spartan, cold even. He wondered what that said about Joy's character. Perhaps she wanted to remain professional here, not let her feelings intrude into her work.

The phone on her desk rang. Chris hesitated for a moment, then reached to answer it. 'Joy Taylor's room. I'm afraid she's not here right now.'

'Barry's Garage here. Can you pass on a message? Her car's ready. If she wants to collect it after six, the keys will be left on the forecourt.'

'I'll tell her.' Just at that minute Joy came back in the room and he passed on the message.

She nodded. 'I'll get it tonight, I'm not leaving till seven. And it's a nuisance, being without a car. Now, let's have a look at this cut.'

Joy peeled off the dressing and inspected the butterfly

stitches underneath. 'You could have had this sutured,' she muttered, 'but butterfly stitches will do. Did you lose much blood?'

'Not a lot,' he said. 'It was more a case of what might have happened than what did happen.'

She shuddered at the thought. 'What might have happened,' she mumbled. But then she regained her confidence. There was a job to be done.

She was a good nurse, gentle and effective. She washed the cut, dusted it with antiseptic powder and then applied fresh butterfly stitches. There was a peculiar intimacy in having her lean over him, her arm brushing his naked chest. He could detect the faintest of perfumes under the strong hospital smell from the dressing. Perhaps it was from her hair. But Joy didn't once look at him. Her attention was fixed on his injury.

'That should do for a while. I don't think you should lift heavy weights for a while. Ask another midwife to...' She stopped when she saw him smiling. 'Is there any point to telling you this?'

'I have been injured before. I know enough not to pull out stitches.'

'Well...you can put your shirt back on now.'

They seemed to have come to some kind of a truce, but there was something he had to tell her. 'I agree that the last thing the hospital needs is publicity. But if asked I'll testify against this man.' His face grew hard as he thought about what had happened. 'You don't back away from threats...ever.'

There was silence between them, then she said, 'I'm sure you're right. Well...you can go now.'

Chris went back to the midwives' station. His shift was already over, and he chatted briefly to the shift leader before leaving. It was a dismal summer's day outside, a heavy rain contrasting with the spell of good weather they had just enjoyed.

After a quiet day spent catching up on lost sleep, he drove back to the hospital and parked where he couldn't be seen but had a view of the exit from the O and G unit. Then he waited.

At ten past seven he saw Joy come out, wrapped in a long coat with the collar up. Head down, she started to pace down the long drive. He waited until she was well past him and then drove after her.

Chris pulled in ahead of her, walked round the car and opened the passenger door. 'I'll give you a lift,' he said.

She looked at him uncertainly. 'There's really no need. I can catch a bus at the gates.'

'You'll not catch a bus straight to Barry's Garage. Get in, it's ridiculous being out in this weather, I'll take you there.'

Still she hesitated.

'You're not afraid of me, are you?' he asked.

Their eyes met in challenge and this, of course, decided her. 'Certainly not!' she snapped, and climbed in.

CHAPTER THREE

'YOU know where Barry's Garage is?' Joy asked as Chris turned out of the hospital gates and set off confidently through a maze of back streets.

'I do now. I looked it up in the street guide.'

A burst of rain rattled on the windscreen and Joy said abstractedly, 'I'm glad I got a lift. I could have taken a taxi but...' Then she realised something. 'You looked it up in the street guide? Why should you?' After a pause she went on, 'It wasn't a coincidence, you coming down the drive, then, was it? You finished work ages ago. You were waiting for me.'

'It wasn't a coincidence and, yes, I was waiting for you. I wanted to talk to you. But if you feel threatened, I'll happily drop you in the middle of this downpour...well, unhappily drop you. You'd get very wet. Do you feel threatened?'

'I feel more angry than threatened. You've manipulated me. What is it that you have to talk about so urgently?'

He hadn't thought this far ahead and knew he'd have to be cautious. Slowly, he said, 'I think you have to get to know the people you work with—and for. And I don't know you yet and you don't know me. All you see in me is a soldier. You don't like the army, do you?'

'Not just the army. The navy and the air force, too.' Her answer was flat and direct.

'Will you tell me why?'

'Not in specific detail,' Joy said coolly. 'It's just that

44

I've seen what the armed forces can do to a person. It makes them hard. Brutalises them.'

'It can do that,' he agreed. 'But it doesn't have to. The army is good for teamwork. Good at finding what qualities a man has, and bringing them out. But I feel you're trying to exclude me from the team. I get on with the other midwives and the mums well enough. But not you. Why is that?'

Chris half expected her to deny his accusations, but she didn't and so she went up in his estimation. 'I just think that…there's something about you I don't know. There was a politician once who attacked her boss in the House of Commons and in effect ruined his career. She said that there was something of the night about him. Well, I feel that there is—or could be—something of the night about you.'

He was silent, he hadn't expected this. Joy was far more shrewd than he'd expected. Or was he more transparent than he'd thought? 'I'll have to think about that,' he said. 'Perhaps you guessed—I've spent a lot of my life working at night.'

'It shows,' she said.

There were roadworks ahead, and a long line of traffic patiently queuing to get through the single lane. He pulled on the handbrake to wait their turn. Perhaps they could talk about something slightly different.

'Have you ever thought that the kind of work you do turns you into a specific kind of person?' he asked. 'I had a friend once who worked as a psychiatric nurse, dealing with some of the worst sociopaths you could wish to meet. He was good at it, even enjoyed it. But after six years he transferred to general nursing. He said that dealing with…evil all the time was starting to affect him.'

Joy looked at him in amazement. 'That's not the kind of remark I expect from an ex-soldier!'

'You're being narrow-minded,' he chided. 'Just think about what I'm saying. Do midwives differ from geriatric nurses or A and E nurses? I think they probably do. And it's their job that changes them.'

Reluctantly she said, 'There could be something in what you say. I'll have to think about it.'

Ahead of them the temporary traffic light changed to green. Chris had to concentrate on weaving the heavy vehicle past pedestrians who apparently thought they could use the road as freely as the pavement. It wasn't far then, and Joy remained silent until they swung into the forecourt of Barry's Garage.

She didn't try to get out. Instead she said, 'I've been thinking about what you said. About how what we do affects how we live and what we believe. Now I know why you came into midwifery. You wanted to change yourself, didn't you?'

Chris was shocked by her astuteness. He had underrated this woman! 'You might be right,' he admitted gruffly.

Although the forecourt was deserted, he had drawn up in a corner where they couldn't easily be seen. Even though there was silence between them she still showed no sign of wanting to get out of his car. Perhaps it was the great fatigue that hit a lot of hospital workers at this time of day. Or perhaps… He said, 'I've enjoyed talking to you, I'd like to talk to you longer. Might I take you to dinner some time quite soon?'

'Take me to dinner? Certainly not! We're not that close, not even friends, I—'

'I think the question is, would you enjoy a civilised meal in pleasant surroundings with me, somewhere well away from the hospital atmosphere? That's all I'm offering. Dinner. And conversation.'

'I must say, conversation with you is a bit... stimulating,' she muttered. 'I suppose your macho pride wouldn't allow me to pay my half?'

'It certainly wouldn't,' he agreed. 'But if it's really a point of principle with you, I would have no objection to you paying for, say, a half-bottle of dessert wine.'

'You're all heart,' Joy said. 'Why d'you want to have dinner with me anyway? Aren't there lots of nurses you could ask?'

'I'm not interested in nurses, I'm interested in you.' Chris looked out of the window at the pouring rain, his face blank. He knew he was taking a risk here. He said, 'When I first saw you, and when I came into your room for that meeting, I felt something that I'd never felt before. Some kind of instant attraction, I suppose. There was a spark that fired between us. I felt it—and I know that you felt it, too.'

'How d'you know that?' she snapped. 'How can you possibly know what I'm thinking? You're imagining any...attraction between us.'

'No, I'm not. I know how you felt because I saw it in your face. Look, I'm trying desperately to be honest here, I'm taking a chance I've never taken before. Can't you do the same?'

There was silence, then Joy took a deep breath and let it out slowly. 'I suppose I am human,' she murmured. 'I've got feelings like anybody else, though I try to keep them at a distance, certainly away from my work. Yes, I did feel something for you.' Her voice became more determined. 'But it was purely physical. Nothing serious. Just like seeing someone you might fancy on TV.'

He knew she wouldn't say any more, that what she had said so far had been an effort. Still, it had been an effort for him as well. 'So, shall we have dinner soon?' he asked.

'I'm free on Friday night. But I don't want all the hospital knowing about this.'

'I know how to be discreet.'

'All right, pick me up at home—say, about eight? I live at 28 Rathbone Road. D'you know it?'

'I'll find it.' Chris walked round to open her door. 'I'll just wait here till I see you in your car.'

She drove out two minutes later, waved to him and was gone.

Chris still didn't know the area too well and on the day before he was due to take Joy to dinner he asked casually about where the best place was to dine locally. All sorts of restaurants and pubs were suggested to him. Eventually he decided on Croston's, a large hotel in Scarborough some ten miles away. The food was supposed to be excellent. He would have preferred somewhere small and intimate, but he thought that might frighten Joy. In his break he phoned to make a reservation.

He'd seen her once or twice since taking her to the garage. They had passed each other in the corridor, exchanging distant smiles. On that day he had heard that she'd gone to a management meeting—by chance he met her coming back from it. She was dressed in a formal black suit and she looked both angry and upset.

'I hope it's not me you're mad at,' Chris said mildly.

'For once, no. I've just been to a management meeting called by the hospital Chief Executive Officer and they're going to…' Joy collected herself and said in a brittle voice, 'Management has to do what it has to do.'

'You could tell me,' he said. 'I know how to keep a secret. I've even been on an army course on how to keep secrets.'

'Then you'll understand if I don't tell you more,' she said tersely.

'Quite. By the way, I've booked us a table at Croston's for tomorrow night.'

'Croston's? I've never been there, it's supposed to be very good. Are you trying to impress me?'

'I would like to impress you,' he said. 'I very much would like to impress you.'

She had no answer to that.

Chris picked Joy up the next evening, still in his four-wheel-drive. He was wearing a lightweight grey suit in fine wool, with a dark blue shirt and plain tie. When it was appropriate, he liked dressing well.

Number 28 Rathbone Road was a pleasant house in a cul-de-sac—a pre-war semi, he thought. It was a larger house than he had anticipated. When he knocked at precisely one minute to eight, she opened the door at once. Obviously she had been waiting for him.

'Let's go,' she said. 'I'll not ask you in, I'd only have to introduce you to my mother, and then she'd be bothering me with questions.'

'I would have quite liked to meet your mother. But perhaps another time.'

She was dressed less formally than he had seen her before, in a white dress with silver and dark blue flashes on it. It was V-necked, cut quite low, showing the swell of her generous breasts. So far he had only seen her in uniform or a formal suit.

'You look very well,' he said. She wasn't sure what to make of that. He handed her into the car and they set off on the twenty-five minute journey down the coast road.

At first Scarborough had been a bit of a maze. It seemed to be built on two levels, so he had spent one evening just driving round, trying to find out what was where. He didn't like not knowing where he was going. 'You've certainly learned your way around,' Joy said.

'It's a good idea to be clear about where you're going and how to get there.'

'Is that a comment about getting through Scarborough or a comment on life in general?'

'It could be both. D'you know where *we're* going, Joy?'

If his words were a challenge, she avoided it. 'You said Croston's. Look, there's the entrance.'

They drew into the forecourt of the hotel, handing the keys of the car to the doorman who would park it. 'We've come by car, we may well go back by taxi,' he said. 'Then we can enjoy a drink.'

'You're not going to drink too much?' Her voice was sharp.

'No. I never drink too much. I don't like losing control.'

They entered the foyer of the hotel, crossed the rich purple carpet to the restaurant door. The *maître d'hôtel* told them that their table would soon be ready, and would they like a drink in the bar first? He conducted them to a table in the adjoining bar.

Chris eyed the ornate carving of the panelling and the rich colours of the upholstery appreciatively. This was an old-fashioned hotel which had managed to keep up with the times. He liked it. It gave a sense of security.

He saw Joy hesitating over the list of drinks, obviously bewildered by the vast selection. 'This is a nice old-fashioned place,' he said. 'Why not have a nice, old-fashioned drink? There's a very good list of sherries here—shall I order you one?'

'Yes, please, if you're having the same. I've never been here before. I rather like it.'

The waiter fetched the two light sherries he had ordered and placed a plate of nuts on the table. They both sipped, both reached for a nut at the same time. Their hands touched—and Joy pulled hers back quickly. 'I'm still not sure what I'm doing here,' she said frostily.

'Let's talk about work first, then. The midwives and the ancillary staff largely make up a very well-organised team. You and the shift leaders work well together, problems are sorted out quickly. There's good communication at all levels. I'll bet you know the backgrounds of every one of your staff, who's good at what.' Chris paused, then leaned forward. 'The midwives accept me. You don't. You're keeping me out of the team.'

'I know,' Joy said. 'I can't help it. You're...different. But I'm trying not to keep you out. It's just me.' She thought for a moment, then said, 'You think we're a good team?'

'Most are very good, one or two are excellent. But in any team there's always one or two who can let the others down.'

'I know. I wish I could...' Then she caught herself. 'I can't discuss other members of my staff with you,' she said primly.

'I should think not,' he said with a grin. After that,

the conversation was more relaxed, and dangerous subjects were avoided.

Soon they were conducted to their table. She told him that she didn't drink much wine, but that she liked something light and white—leibfraumilch? He hoped she didn't see him wince. Chris ordered a bottle of vintage Chablis which he knew well. There had been a catch that day, so after a starter of deep fried goat's cheese and salad, they both had a fish main course with bundles of steamed vegetables.

'I'm surprised you ordered fish, like me,' Joy said impishly. 'I would have thought you were a big red-meat eater.'

'I like meat. But the fish from the North Sea is the best I've ever tasted.'

He glanced round the large dining room, saw the well-dressed diners, the careful staff, heard the hushed voices. Then he smiled at her. 'I'm enjoying myself. We're having an excellent meal, I'm in the company of an attractive and intelligent woman and I'm looking forward to talking to you.'

He tried to remain imperturbable as she looked at him thoughtfully, running her tongue over her bottom lip. Such a soft, curved lip!

'I'm looking forward to talking to you, too. We'll sit here and both enjoy our meal. And you can tell me the real reason you became a midwife.'

'I thought I already had,' he said in some surprise.

'Yes. You gave some nice bland reasons, and I suspect all of them are true. But there's an awful lot more to what you've told me. Isn't there?'

Chris looked at her with growing respect, and just a little apprehension. 'You're very perceptive,' he said, 'and that makes you seem quite formidable.'

'So tell me.'

He thought a while, aware that she was watching him, also aware that as he thought his face got harder, more bleak.

'I need to know you better first,' he said eventually, 'but I think I will in time. Now, let's just enjoy the meal.'

In fact, they were enjoying the meal, enjoying each other's company. But both were fencing—trying to get a little advantage, trying to work out what the other was thinking. It was stimulating.

They finished their meal with a plain but delicious ice cream and went back into the bar for coffee. They were seated in a banquette, side by side instead of facing each other. Chris was aware of the touch of her against him, of the warmth of her thigh and her arm. He could smell her perfume now, just the faintest of scents. He put his hand over hers and the shock took him again.

They looked at each other, silently at first. 'You felt it,' he said.

'Yes,' Joy said simply, 'I felt it. But I'll have to fight against it. It's something I just have to cope with.' Slowly, she moved her hand from under his.

'What exactly have you against the military mind?' he asked after a while. 'I know its strengths and weaknesses and I'd be interested to see if you agree with me.'

She shrugged. 'My father was in the Royal Navy. A career officer. So I saw very little of him as a child, he was a bit remote. I think the navy was my father's life, when it should have been his family.'

'It happens,' Chris conceded. 'But there's more, isn't there?'

'Why am I telling you all this? I don't usually tell people and anyway you're my...'

'I'm one of your subordinates,' he said with a grin.

He saw her face colour, and laughed. 'Don't worry, you know very well I'm not going to gossip about you.'

'Yes, I suppose I do,' she said. 'And I don't see anyone as my subordinate. I...'

There was a burst of raucous male laughter from behind them, unusually loud in the hushed bar. Chris turned to look, then faced her, his face hard.

'I'm sorry,' he said. 'I suspect what has been a very pleasant evening is going to be spoiled. Perhaps not.'

Joy looked at him, perplexed. 'Why...? What...?'

He explained. 'The noisy group over there is, I suspect, a set of drug-company representatives. Dr Trust is with them, he's just spotted us and he's not very happy. And he's coming over.'

Joy turned her head to look. She obviously noted the aggressive way Henry Trust was making his way towards them. 'Oh, dear,' she said. 'I hope there isn't going to be any kind of scene. You may have heard that Henry's the man I've been...seeing a little of.'

'I know,' said Chris. 'But there'll be no problem with any kind of confrontation.'

As he got closer they both realised that Henry was drunk. His walk was slightly unsteady, his eyes glassy. Chris knew that if it was a drug company that was entertaining, then money would be no object. Henry would have drunk as much as he wished.

Henry came to their table, swaying slightly. 'This is a nice sight,' he said. 'Having a good time with the staff, are we, Joy?'

Chris saw that Joy wasn't going to be spoken to like that. 'I'm having a very good time, thank you, Henry,' she said. 'Chris has brought me out to dinner and we've had a wonderful meal.'

'How nice. Well, d'you mind if my friends and I join you? Perhaps I can buy you a drink—or they can anyway.' He put his glass on the table and turned to wave to the little group.

'I mind if you join us,' said Chris, 'I mind very much.'

Henry turned back, looked disbelievingly at Chris. 'Remember who you are,' he said thickly. 'I'm not talking to you.'

Chris stood, leaned a little closer to Henry. 'I know who I am,' he said softly, 'and now I'm talking to you. Go back and join your drunken, oafish friends. Or I'll have the management throw you out.'

The two stared at each other, then Henry broke eye contact. 'I don't know what you think you're saying,' he blustered. 'I just came over to say hello to a colleague and I—'

'You've said hello,' Chris interrupted. 'Now Joy and I would like to carry on with our conversation.'

Henry turned in desperation to Joy. 'Joy, are you going to—?'

'I think it for the best if you rejoin your friends, Henry,' she said.

Henry stood there a moment longer, looking from one to the other, then turned and silently went back to his group.

'I really am sorry,' Chris said. 'I hope it didn't spoil your evening too much.'

'It wasn't your fault,' she sighed. 'But I have been out with him once or twice. Perhaps he thought that he has some sort of…rights over me.'

Then, half-angrily, she said, 'But you didn't leave

him anywhere to go, did you? No chance to make a dignified withdrawal.'

'No point in trying,' said Chris. 'The mood he was in, he'd take any attempt at reason as a sign of weakness.'

Joy remained silent a moment. Then she sighed. 'I guess you're right,' she said. 'But didn't you think that as he's a doctor he could harm you professionally?'

Chris frowned, thinking. 'I'm a midwife. In a delivery room, I'm technically in charge—not the doctor. If a doctor—especially one like Henry—thinks he can bully me, then my work and the welfare of my patients suffer.'

She looked at him, amazed. 'Sometimes you baffle me,' she said. 'You obviously meant what you said. I think that you're just a hard man and then you come out with something sensitive like that. How can you be both people?'

He looked pensive. 'I think,' he said, 'that if there's going to be some kind of confrontation you have to read a person quickly, decide whether to offer something, try to be reasonable or to threaten. And you have to decide—not just hope the situation will resolve itself.'

That intrigued her. 'You're not just trying to impress me, are you?' she asked. 'That's the way you want to behave.'

'That's the way I try to behave. But, of course, I'm not always successful. Now, let's change the subject and you can tell me why you decided to move from being a nurse to being a midwife.'

'Why d'you want to change the subject?'

He ticked off the answers. 'One, because I want a calm, pleasant evening. Two, I'm very interested in you. Shall I pour you more coffee?'

After that their evening was more relaxed. Joy told him about what it had been like growing up in Ransome, about how she'd gone away to train in Leeds and Sheffield. Chris told her something of his own training in London, of how he'd decided finally to make a break from the city.

Then they asked for a new pot of coffee, and she was surprised when she saw how late it was. 'We'd better go soon,' she said. 'I'm not usually out so late.'

'As you wish. I've really enjoyed myself.'

Chris had watched his alcohol intake, and decided it was quite safe for him to drive. He negotiated his way out of the town. There was quite a lot of noise, it was Friday night and the pubs were throwing out. 'Friday night,' Joy sighed. 'You know I used to work on A and E? This and Saturday evenings were always our busiest times.'

He nodded. 'I can guess.'

On the outskirts of town they turned a corner by a pub and saw a police car drawn up. A policeman and a policewoman were apparently arguing with a small, noisy crowd. There was a body lying on the ground. People were walking by on the other side of the road; no cars were stopping. Chris cursed softly, and drew up some distance away.

'What are you doing?' Joy asked. 'This is no business of ours.'

'That woman police officer. She's the one that interviewed me. She was good, I liked her. And it looks like she could use a little help at the moment.'

'Are you going to start fighting again?'

'I hope not. But three people are often better than two. That crowd doesn't really want trouble, they're just being pushed on by alcohol.'

'But, like I said, it's none of your business!'

'It is in that someone I know is in trouble. And you never walk away from trouble, Joy. It always follows you. You stay here, you'll be quite safe.'

'If you're getting out then I'm following you. Now, don't argue.'

He had done this kind of thing before. He walked over boldly, easing people out of his way. 'Excuse me! Let me through, this is important.' One or two people might have objected but they looked at the size of him, the broad shoulders and the determination of the face, and decided to say nothing.

With the WPC was a much younger policeman, obviously not long out of training. Chris realised that he was still not sure what to do. He was arguing with a group—not a good idea with a set of drunkards.

Chris got to the front of the little group. 'Stand back now,' he shouted. 'Medical assistance here.' He walked to the largest man, who appeared to be causing the most trouble, bent forward till their two heads were only inches apart and shouted again, 'I said move! Medical assistance here.'

It was the words 'medical assistance' that did it. The man stood for a moment longer, and then moved back. And somehow the fight went out of the crowd.

Thinking that he ought to show some signs of really bringing medical aid, Chris turned to the figure on the floor. But Joy was already stooping there, gently easing the man onto his side. So Chris walked over to have a word with his policewoman friend and her colleague. 'Nice to see you again, WPC Ralston,' he said.

She looked at him. 'Would you like to stop being a midwife and work in the police?' she asked. 'You've got the voice for it.'

'Just thought I'd stop for a chat,' said Chris.

'Glad you did. Things were getting a bit overheated here.' She turned to the crowd. 'Come along now, folk, the show's over. I can hear the ambulance coming so move along, please!'

Slowly, regretfully, the crowd started to drift away. And in the distance Chris could hear the sound of a siren.

'It was good of you to lend a hand,' said the young policeman, 'but we were doing all right.'

'I know that,' said Chris. 'We just wanted to see if you needed any medical aid. D'you want to look at this man on the ground?'

'I've been on our first-aid course,' the young policeman said curtly. 'I know what to do.'

'I'm sure you do.' Chris was soothing. He could tell the man was inexperienced, still a little unnerved by what had just happened. 'I know the course, it's a good one. But, if you like, I'll go over what you learned. A bit of revision.'

He pointed out how Joy had eased him over, how she had checked to see that the man hadn't swallowed his tongue. 'Remember, check ABC. Airways, breathing, circulation. If the airway is clear, if he's breathing, if his heart is beating, then the chances are you can leave him till the experts come to move him. Oh, and you could add heavy bleeding to that list.'

'I remember all that,' said the young policeman, 'but I appreciate the revision.'

Suddenly the scene was lit by two sets of flashing lights, an ambulance and a police car arriving practically at the same time. There seemed to be an excess of men in uniform—all of them big.

'These two have been giving me a hand,' the policewoman said. 'Old friends of mine.' She smiled up at Chris. 'I'm still thinking of having that second kid.'

'I recommend it,' said Chris. 'Keep in touch.' And he and Joy walked back to the car.

'Will this happen every time I go out with you?' asked Joy. 'Two fights in one night? I don't think I can stand the pace.'

'Come on,' said Chris, 'when you worked in A and E you must have had nights much worse than this.'

'Well, yes. But seeing it actually on the street—it's made my heart beat faster.'

'And I thought it was being with me. I'm disappointed.'

'That's life, Chris.' She drummed her fingers on the dashboard, then said, 'I had a bit of a chat with your policewoman friend. She said that if she'd been a bit younger, and didn't have a kid and wasn't happily married, she could really fancy you.'

'Well, there's a recommendation. WPC Ralston is a woman of taste.'

'She also asked me if it was serious between us. I said no and she said to grab you while I could.'

'And you said?'

'I said I'd consider it. What I didn't say was that what I didn't really want was someone who attracted trouble like you do.'

'That's unfair,' he said.

They were well out of Scarborough now, driving along the road that ran near the coast. Suddenly he turned the car and bumped down a narrow lane. 'Where are we going?' she asked, half curious, half apprehensive.

'This is near where I live. I come down here a lot.

It's the best way to the seaside and I love it. D'you know the road?'

'Of course I do. I've picnicked down here. But never at night.'

'At night it's different, you'll see.'

They arrived at the end of the road, where there was just enough space for a couple of cars to park on the verge. Chris came round to help Joy out. The night was warm, full of the conflicting scents of sea and sun-warmed hay.

They weren't dressed for a midnight walk, so he led her along the path, perhaps fifty yards, to where there was an old wooden bench, perched high on the cliff edge. They sat together, saying nothing, enjoying the sound of the sea rustling below, looking towards the horizon where two distinct shades of dark blue met. Occasionally there was a flash of phosphorescence and the dim lights of a passing ship.

'I think I've enjoyed myself tonight,' Joy said after a while, 'though I didn't really expect to. I came out to get you settled in my mind, to work out what I really think of you, what you're really like. But I'm even less sure than before. There's one side of you—the side that dealt with Henry, that helped the police. I'm not sure I like that bit, even though it might be the real you. And then—I think—there's another side.'

Chris put his arms round her, gently pulled her to him and kissed her. 'That I like,' she said. 'I like you, I don't like you and I can't keep away from you. What are we going to do?'

'For once,' he said, 'I'll say wait and see. Other than that, I don't know what to do either.'

'Will you kiss me again? And then perhaps you'd better take me home.'

*   *   *

That night, in bed alone, Chris had the nightmare again. He woke at four o'clock in the morning and after a while he decided he didn't want to wait and see what was to happen between Joy and him. But what else could he do?

CHAPTER FOUR

CHRIS didn't go to the hospital barbecue. Tricia Patton had phoned him to say she had met a man who very much wanted to take her, and since he didn't drink they could go in his car. She hoped Chris didn't mind.

'No trouble,' Chris told her. 'You have a good time, I'm sure you'll enjoy yourself. I don't think I'll bother to go.'

'We could have had a good time together,' Tricia said, a little wistfully.

'You will anyhow. And I think this new man of yours is a very lucky fellow. See you, Tricia.'

So that little problem had sorted itself out. Good, he had other things to worry about.

He had that Saturday off, so first he just pottered round the house. This didn't satisfy him so he changed and went for a run along the much loved clifftops. And as he ran, he thought.

He considered phoning Joy. Then he decided against it. He wasn't sure where their relationship was going, but he was certain that the next step would have to come from her. He didn't like not being able to do anything, having to wait for someone else to make up their mind. But that's how it was.

One thing was certain. He was more attracted to her than ever. On Friday night he'd got to know her a little better. Underneath that apparently aloof exterior he had glimpsed an exciting and passionate woman.

* * *

On Sunday he went into work, the delivery suite as usual. When he took over his patient, Ellie Sutton was in the first stage of labour. At first she was a little surprised to see a male midwife, but she soon got used to it and then they got on fine. Ellie's husband was a soldier. He was abroad and couldn't be present for the birth. When Chris told her that he, too, had been a soldier, they got on even better.

After about an hour Chris noticed that the electronic foetal monitor, attached to Ellie's abdomen, showed that the baby's heart was slowing a little. He was pretty sure that this meant nothing, but protocol dictated that he call the doctor on duty and so he did so.

Five minutes later Henry Trust walked into the room. He nodded coldly to Chris, walked over and looked at the notes Chris had made. 'What seems to be the problem, Midwife?' he asked.

Henry was the doctor in charge, and Chris had to work with him. Neutrally, Chris explained what had happened.

'I see,' said Henry. Only then did he walk over to the figure on the couch and say hello to the patient.

After the examination Henry decided that there was nothing yet to worry about—just what Chris had anticipated. He thought that Henry would then have left—the man didn't usually spend more time than he had to in the delivery room. But Henry didn't leave. Instead he sat by the wall, reading from a textbook and occasionally coming to see how Ellie's labour was progressing. Chris did his usual work.

Finally the baby was about to be born, and Chris asked Henry if he wanted to act as assistant.

'No,' said Henry. 'Get someone from the midwives'

station.' So Chris phoned for an assistant, and shortly afterwards Ellie had a perfect little boy.

Henry still remained in the room, but distanced himself from the proceedings. He took one cursory look at the baby, nodded again to Chris and said, 'Fine'. He didn't congratulate the mother.

Chris said nothing but carried on with the usual procedures—the Apgar score, the tests and readings. He told Ellie that she had a wonderful baby—which was true. Then the porter came to take mother and baby to the postnatal ward. Ellie squeezed Chris's hand and said thank you.

Chris and Henry were now alone in the delivery room.

'Did you enjoy your meal on Friday evening?' Henry asked.

'Very much so. I enjoyed both the meal and the company. I hope you had a good time, too?'

Henry said nothing. He scowled at Chris, and slammed out of the door. Chris shrugged. The man might be a tolerable clinical doctor, but he had a lot to learn about patient care.

At morning break on Monday there was a note in his pigeonhole. 'Please ring when it is convenient for you to see me, J. Taylor.' The shift leader said that now was fine for him to go as there was nothing to do for the next half-hour.

Joy's voice was cold on the phone. 'I think we need to talk—can you come now?'

'I've just arranged it. I'm on my way,' said Chris. He wondered why Joy had sounded so remote.

She didn't return his smile when he entered her room. Instead she gestured to a chair facing her desk. 'Please, sit down. We have something rather difficult to discuss.'

He sat, facing her across her desk, his face impassive.

She seemed to have some difficulty in speaking, but eventually she said, 'First of all, Chris, I want you to know I enjoyed Friday night. It was a very pleasant evening. But it can't happen again. It's not wise. I've always been against…short-term sexual relationships at work. It can so easily lead to problems.'

'Especially when you're my superior,' Chris pointed out, expressionlessly. 'Incidentally, who said anything about our relationship being short term? I think you know me enough by now to realise that it's you that I'm interested in. I want to know you longer and better. I'm not just looking for quick sexual gratification. And what are the problems?'

'I'm saying the relationship is short term and the problem is Dr Trust. He came in to see me earlier this morning.' Joy seemed to be having difficulty in getting her thoughts straight. 'Dr Trust apologised if he upset me on Friday. But he was surprised to see me going out with another man. He said he felt that we two had an understanding and that if I was to go out with someone else, the least I could do was mention it to him.' Unhappily, Joy pushed papers around her desk. 'Our relationship was not that close, but maybe he has a point.'

She looked directly at Chris. 'Have you nothing to say?'

He thought for a moment. 'Your past or present relationship with Dr Trust is none of my business,' he said eventually. 'I can give you my opinion of him if you wish, but what you feel is the most important thing.'

'Perhaps so. Anyway he apologised to me for his behaviour. He said he had been led astray by those representatives from the drug company. Perhaps he has an excuse.'

'A very poor one,' said Chris. 'A man chooses whether he wants to drink or not. It's entirely his own decision and he's responsible for the consequences.'

Joy smiled, very faintly. 'There are some things that you're absolutely implacable about, aren't there?' she asked. 'I don't know whether it's a character trait that I like or I don't like.'

Her face became severe again. 'Anyway, you and Dr Trust had to work together on Sunday afternoon. You were on duty, he was the resident doctor.'

'Yes. There was a query over the foetal heart rate so I called for him. He was in the delivery room for a good two hours.'

'Quite. Dr Trust says that he was willing to be professional, to ignore what had happened, but that you were uncooperative, awkward, truculent and in general hard to deal with. He said this kind of behaviour isn't easy to prove, but he didn't like it and he doesn't see any reason why he should put up with it.'

'It may be not easy to prove,' said Chris calmly, 'but it's also hard to disprove. Have you talked to the woman in the delivery room—Ellie Sutton?'

'No. Dr Trust particularly said that he didn't want me questioning people. This wasn't a formal complaint. But he wanted me to understand how he felt. Perhaps I should have a word with you. Which I'm doing.'

Chris was silent for a moment. Then he said, 'Since I'm not accused of anything specific, I can't defend myself. So I won't even try. Now you've got to think about his behaviour, which you must have observed over the past few weeks. You may have had reports about him. Then you've got to compare that with what you know

of me, and the reports you've had of me. Then make
up your mind and decide who's telling the truth.'

'But I know you! You can be really hard!'

'In the room where a mother is giving birth? Possibly,
Joy.' He stood, smiled at her. 'Now I'm going to leave
you to make up your mind. You will let me know what
you decide, won't you? Remember, I did promise that
if you weren't satisfied after six months, I'd leave.'

'Chris, you've got to offer me something. An argument, a defence, just something! You can't leave me
like this!'

'I can leave you. I have to. This is the loneliness of
power. You're in power, you have to make decisions.
But I know you'll do a good job. Now, I'd better get
back to work.'

There was no word from Joy all through the afternoon. He carried on with his work, enjoyed it as usual.
But when he drove home he felt slightly desolate. He'd
thought she would have been in touch.

After a quick tea he decided he had to get out of the
house. He didn't want a run, he'd walk. So he took his
favourite route, down the little road and onto the coast
path. He passed the seat where he'd been with Joy on
Friday evening, then scrambled down a low part of the
cliff onto a little beach of stones. It was another glorious
evening as he sat there and waited for peace.

At first he threw stones into the water, an aimless but
strangely satisfying pursuit. And slowly the turmoil inside him calmed.

What *was* he to do about Joy? He thought again about
the relationships he'd had in his life so far. All very
pleasant, all fine for a while. But ultimately unsatis-
fying. He thought that Joy would give him far more.
And he could give her far more, too.

Behind him he heard the rattle of stones slipping, then the regular crunch of steps. Not many people came down here, but there was a way to the beach. He turned. It was Joy. He wasn't surprised, there seemed to be something of the inevitable about it.

She was dressed casually, like himself, in blue jeans, a white T-shirt and a darker shirt over the top. Her figure looked well in the outfit.

He stood. They looked at each other, neither smiling, neither surprised. 'This isn't a coincidence?' he asked.

'No. I went to your house. The car was there, but you weren't. I remembered you said you often came down here so I came down myself.'

'So you wanted to see me?'

Joy shook her head as if puzzled. 'I don't think "wanted" is the right word. I *had* to see you. And I very much didn't want to talk to you in hospital. I needed somewhere, just us...no work involved.'

Chris nodded. 'That makes sense. Why don't we sit down? It's calming here. We can talk when you're ready.'

So they sat, side by side but not touching. They listened to the crashing of the waves and then the rattle of the stones pulled by the undertow. In the distance was the buzz of a tractor collecting hay.

'I don't suppose you *are* going just to disappear?' she asked. 'My life was simpler before you came.'

'No, I'm not going to disappear. And you can't hope that problems will just go away. They stay and haunt you. Remember the two saddest words in English are "if only".'

'I know that.' She stopped staring out to sea, turned to look at him. 'You make me think. Sometimes you talk like an expert about running away from things. Are you sure you're not running away from something your-self?'

It had happened again! This woman could detect in him things that no one else had ever discovered. And now he could tell by her air of expectancy that she had read his dismay in his face.

When he didn't reply she went on, 'Are you sure you're not just waiting to get back into the army?'

This he could answer easily. 'I'm in the Reserves, of course. But I was invalided out. I have a limp. I can do easily anything that civilian life might demand—but the particular section of the army that I was involved with needs complete fitness.'

'Just how did you get injured? It wasn't in your ap-plication form.'

'I'll tell you one day.' Chris knew he was being curt, but she was getting too close.

'Are you sure you're not running from something?'

'Possibly I am,' he said. 'Perhaps everyone is running from something. But I don't know, or I'm not sure, what I'm running to. Why did you come to find me?'

She didn't appear to object to his sudden change of subject. 'I thought about what you said this morning. Then I asked myself what I'd think if Henry had ac-cused one of my girls of the same thing. Then I decided I believed you, not Henry. I called him, told him I wouldn't be seeing any more of him socially. I further told him that I had investigated his complaint and would have to insist that any further complaint was in writing, through official channels and was handed first to David Garner.'

'I'll bet he didn't like that,' Chris said.

'Not very much. He tried to bluster, of course, said I was mesmerised by you. He must think I'm a pushover. I told him I'd dropped in to see the woman who had the baby—Ellie Sutton. Her version of events was quite different from his.' She paused a moment. 'I'll try to arrange that you don't have to work with him in future.'

'No need,' said Chris. 'He isn't incompetent at his job. Just doesn't have very good people skills. I can keep a low profile, I promise I won't provoke him. You know that's true, don't you?'

'Yes,' she said. 'It's one of the extraordinary things about you. Anyway, I don't think Henry will be any more trouble. He's running scared now.'

There was another silence. He wriggled closer to her, put an arm round her shoulders. At first Joy tensed, but then he felt her muscles relaxing, and she leaned her head on him.

'You didn't come here to talk about Henry Trust, did you?' he asked.

'No. I wanted to talk about us. I want to understand myself.'

He kissed her gently on the forehead. Under his arm he could feel her relaxing even more, her body resting against his. But then she jerked upright, reluctantly dragged herself away from him.

'Please, don't kiss me or anything because I couldn't stop you and I've got to get sorted out first. I've never felt about anyone the way I feel about you. I've walked past doors, peering in, hoping to see you. When I meet you I get this feeling in the pit of my stomach, it's a great ache of longing, and it's just not me.'

'Join the club,' he said. 'You're not alone. I feel the same way about you.'

'But it's just physical! Just animal attraction! You're not the kind of man I like! I've only ever been out with small men, quiet men. In lots of ways Henry suited me better than you. You stand there like a giant. If anything gets in your way you just sweep it aside. It's the military way of doing things and I don't like it!'

'I am what I am,' he said. 'Can't you take me just as a midwife?'

Joy didn't answer. Suddenly her arms were round his waist, her head on his chest. He lay back, cradling her, stroking her hair, feeling the heaving of her chest as she sobbed. There was nothing he could think of to say.

After a while the sobbing stopped. 'Sorry,' she said, her voice muffled. 'Take it as a bit of woman's weakness. It's pointless. Blame it on the menstrual cycle or something like that.'

Chris continued stroking. 'It's probably not a good idea to bring the subject up again,' he said, 'but I've heard some of my strongest soldiers cry. It depends on the circumstances.'

'Have you ever cried since you were a child?'

Chris remained silent.

'I thought not. Don't preach to me about how weak you really are, I don't believe it. Have you got a handkerchief I could borrow?'

Quietly he offered her one. She wiped away her tears, shook herself and sat upright. 'Well, I haven't got anywhere,' she said, 'but I feel better.'

He looked down at her, and she smiled wanly. So he kissed her again, gently at first, holding her like a tiny bird, letting her know that she could escape at any moment. Yet again he felt the tension melt from her body, the muscles relax. Joy leaned against him, pushed her hand inside his jacket and then pulled at his shirt so that the buttons opened and she could slide her fingers over the warmth of his chest. Now he was lying back and she was resting half on top of him.

In his turn he slid his hand up her back, under the T-shirt felt the roughness of her bra strap. It was easy to undo. With both hands he felt the softness of her skin, stroking her shoulders, her sides. Then his hands came to her front, cupped the fullness of her breasts. He felt her sigh—with pleasure or shock he didn't know. Under the insistent pressure her felt her nipples harden, heard her breathing grow slower, deeper. He kissed her, harder now, and her lips parted under his passion.

For perhaps ten minutes they lay there. He didn't know what would happen next, what they would do. For the moment he was content. Then she sighed, gently pushed him away and sat up.

'Whatever else we might want to do,' she said, 'I'm not going to do it in daylight, in public and on a stony beach. I've…never done this kind of thing before and I think I'd better stop it before we do something that we might regret.'

'I think you're wonderful,' he said, 'you know that. And I doubt I'd regret anything.'

Joy reached behind her, bent forward to fasten her bra. 'Will you kiss me once more and then stay here till I get in my car and drive away?' she asked.

'If that's what you want. But I need to know. Is this an end or a beginning?'

She shook her head, perplexed. 'I still don't know,' she said.

Three days later Joy was still wondering what she should do. And then something happened that threw her completely, made her see Chris in an entirely different light.

She knew he was now working lates. He wasn't meant to be, but he'd agreed to come in as a favour to the shift leader as they were very short-handed. One nurse was on holiday, and yet again Di Owen had phoned in sick.

Joy hadn't spoken to him since their meeting on the beach. She was waiting till her chaotic thoughts had sorted themselves out. The physical attraction to him was so great!

After she had left him she had gone home and showered before going to bed. To her dismay, as she'd smoothed soap over her body, her breasts had tensed, almost as if in memory of the stroking of his hands. How could she deal with a man who could do that to her?

She could see his good points. He appeared kind, generous, thoughtful. But she knew that just below the surface there was that soldier-like attitude of mind, that readiness to take on whatever stood in his way. A soldier was trained to fight.

Of course, many of the qualities that made him a good soldier made him a good midwife. There was the ability to work in a team, the readiness to work longer or odd hours, the willingness to do any job no matter how unpleasant. The shift leaders all wanted him to work for them.

'Is it his sex appeal?' Joy had asked, half joking.

'That's what it was at first,' Alice McKee had said breezily, 'but now it's just that he's a fantastic worker.' The other two had grumbled their agreement.

Joy hadn't had a good day. There had been yet another management meeting and she'd been asked to make yet more cuts in her budget. It was impossible! She was relying on the goodwill of her staff far too much already. David Garner had supported her totally in the early part of the meeting but then some medical emergency had called him away.

Now she sat in her room, looking at schedules, budgets, timetables. It was late at night, she should go home but... Where could she make economies? She was supposed to be a midwife, not an expert in finance. But the course she had been to in London had shown her that the two had to go together.

She knew at times that the NHS had been inefficient. Money had been wasted, lost to greedy contractors and even medical staff. She recalled a technician who had negotiated a very generous call-out rate. If he was called out at night, it was only fair that he should be paid well. But then it was discovered that he was doing three or four assays in one trip—and claiming the call-out fee for each one of them. In an evening he earned as much as she did in a week—and he was paid his salary, too.

However... She decided to go for a walk, see how her unit was functioning. Part of her brain told her that she was hoping for a glimpse of Chris. Perhaps they could even have a coffee together.

But the minute Joy walked down to the staffroom she knew that something was wrong. There was something about the faces of the people who rushed past her, about the way they walked. There was something in the atmosphere.

Then she saw Chris. He was coming towards her, his white uniform covered with far more blood than she thought necessary. She didn't like the way he looked at her, as if he registered that she was there but that she held no interest for him at all.

'What's happening, Chris?' she asked.

He didn't stop to talk to her and she had to trot along-

side him, listening to what he had to say. 'We've got
an emergency. Young woman, seven months pregnant,
knocked down by a drunken driver. We're trying to get
her stabilised before she goes to Theatre for a section.
I'm going to change into scrubs. At the moment it
doesn't look like she'll make it.'

When they reached the staffroom she noted a uni-
formed policeman, sitting uncomfortably, drinking coffee. Automatically her eyes flicked to the noticeboard
that showed who was working where. They were
busy—overstretched, in fact. No time now to worry
about what was wrong with Chris. 'I'll get changed and
come and lend a hand,' she said.

In fact, when she got changed, she found they were
coping—just. So she told the shift leader she was available and went into the room where Chris and David
were. The room seemed over-full. There was David
Garner, his registrar, an anaesthetist, a paediatrician,
Chris and an orderly. They were all gathered round the
still form on the bed. Chris, as midwife, was monitoring
the unborn baby, studying the monitor that had been
wheeled to the side of the bed.

'Foetal heart now stopped,' she heard Chris say.

'Mother's vital signs finished,' added the anaesthetist.
'David, we've done everything possible. There was only
ever the slimmest of chances, you know that. There's
nothing else we can do.'

The flat words echoed round the room. *Nothing else
we can do.* But they all stayed where they were, silently
looking down.

'We did everything we could, but it wasn't enough,'
said David eventually. 'Thank you, everybody.'

Somehow the team spirit dissolved. What two
minutes before had been a closely knit band of people,

working desperately together to a common aim, now became a set of individuals.

'I suppose I'd better go see that policeman,' David went on. 'Then it's my job to see the relations, if there are any.'

Joy saw Chris pick up the woman's left hand and place it on top of her. She was amazed at the gentleness with which he handled it. 'No wedding ring,' he said. 'So apparently she's not married. Of course, she might have a partner.' His voice was thick.

'The police will have to sort that out,' David said. 'I'll see whoever comes.'

For a moment no one spoke. The only sound was the click as Chris switched off the monitor. But that click echoed through the room.

Joy had seen deaths in hospital often enough before. She had even seen one or two in the O and G section, but they were now very rare. Most of the work in her section was happy—mothers had babies and the staff felt that a good job had been well done when they went out into the world. So the sense of desolation in the room was natural. But there were things to do. There were detailed reports to be compiled and the coroner would have to be informed.

Alice McKee put her head round the door, then came in. She didn't need to be told what had happened, she could tell by the way people were standing.

'All right,' she said, 'I'll see to everything in here now. You lot look as if you could do with a rest.'

Individually, people started to leave the room. The work of the hospital had to go on.

Joy found herself walking down the corridor side by side with Chris. He still felt distant, as if she meant nothing to him. 'We did all we could,' she said. 'Every-

one tried. But now and again you just don't succeed.'
When he didn't reply, she asked, 'Are you all right?'

'Well, it's not a nice time for anyone, is it?'

She was surprised at the venom of his reaction. 'It
wasn't anyone you knew, was it?' she persisted.

'No. Just a body off the street. Another kid never
getting born. Just a statistic now. Sorry, Joy, I've got
things to do. I'll see you some time.' And he was off,
striding down the corridor. She blinked as he went.

She glanced in at the midwives' station—as so often
happened things had quietened rapidly. There was now
no need for her. So she went to her room and changed
back into her suit. She knew she should go home, get
to bed. Instead, she made herself a coffee and sat down.

She needed to think about Chris. Having someone die
on the table was rare, upsetting. But nurses, midwives
had to learn how to keep some kind of distance. Joy
had seen young nurses in tears, heard them complain
that it wasn't fair, they just couldn't cope with pain and
death. But they did learn how to cope—and still be able
to feel for their patients. She would have thought that
by this time Chris had learned, too. In fact, with his
military background, Chris should have been able to
cope more easily than most. But, under the granite mask
that was Chris's face, just for once she thought that she
had seen a look of almost unendurable agony. Why had
he taken it so hard?

Joy filed and stacked her papers, finished her drink,
did the little chores around her office that never seemed
to get finished. Then she realised she was deliberately
wasting time. So she went out onto the unit again.

A couple of midwives were sitting quietly in the station. News of the death had obviously spread to everyone and there was a darkness of spirit in the room. 'You

OK, Joy?' one of them asked. She obviously knew Joy had been in the room when it had happened.

'You get used to it,' Joy said, telling the accepted lie, 'though it's a bit hard at times. Anyone seen Chris McAlpine?'

'Just went out two minutes ago. Said he fancied a breath of fresh air. We can beep him if you want.'

'Not important, it'll wait.'

But she went outside anyhow. For a moment she remembered that this was what Janet Fell had done, but the memory didn't worry her. She would be all right.

Tonight there was a full moon, and ahead of her she could see a white-clad figure walking through the trees. She set off after it. The figure didn't seem to be going anywhere specific. It was an aimless walk, the only point being to keep moving. She soon caught up.

'Chris, it's me—Joy. Have you got a minute?'

'Of course. Am I needed back on the unit?' She should have known. His voice was as calm, as controlled as ever.

'No, you're not needed on the unit. There's a seat there, could we sit down? I'd like to talk to you.'

'Certainly, if you wish.' He walked to the bench and sat, stared straight ahead as she sat by him.

That was it. She felt he was remote, an incalculable distance from her. He didn't care if she sat by him or not. At the moment she wasn't important to him. He was fighting some inner demon. 'Yes?' he asked.

Joy took a breath. This was going to be harder than she had thought. Sitting half under a tree, they were in shadow and she had no means of reading Chris's face. All he was to her was a white blur. She bit her lip, reached out and took his hand. He didn't react. But he didn't let go.

'You and me,' she said. 'We keep things from each other. We need more honesty, more openness. Now, tell me why you were so upset about that mother and baby dying. We know it happens. And you must have seen death before.'

'Oh, yes,' he said. 'I've seen people die, I've even seen friends die.'

'I'm talking about in hospital,' she said. 'We do what we can, we do a lot, but there comes a time when that's not enough. Mothers and babies can die. Now, can we stop fencing? Will you tell me about...why you were so upset?' Defiantly, she squeezed his hand.

'Why should I tell you? Aren't my problems my own?'

'No. You should know that I've got some... emotional investment in you. In spite of myself, I've got to know you. I think perhaps I even love you. And, Chris McAlpine, I've never ever said that to a man before. Now, please?'

He lifted his arm, turned his wrist to look at his watch. The luminous dial flashed in the dark.

'You don't need to go back yet,' she urged. 'Tell me. Why were you so upset? Chris, I've got to know!'

'One reason is that I never knew my mother—she died, having me. Eclampsia. No special reason, you know that. I was brought up by my father and I couldn't have had a better parent. He never remarried and we were happy together. But I often wished I had a mother.'

I often wished I had a mother. Joy thought it was the most desolate thing she had ever heard Chris say. She felt a great wave of love and compassion for this man, who sometimes seemed so hard and yet underneath felt and suffered as everyone did. Her own relationship with her father hadn't been ideal—but at least she'd had a mother.

Still…she wasn't yet convinced. 'There's more, isn't there? Can't you tell me it all?'

She felt, rather than saw, him shake his head. 'One day I will, one day quite soon. But I can't now, it's a bit too close. I was trying to help a woman have a baby. Out in the field. She and the baby died because of a miscalculation on my part.'

'But were you a midwife? Why do you think that—?'

They both heard it—his beeper rang. 'Work calls, I'm needed back on the unit,' he said.

'But there's a lot we have to talk about still!'

Chris stood, and she had to stand, too. When he spoke she could hear the smile in his voice and she relaxed slightly. 'You know very well that work comes first. Come on, you can walk back with me.' And together they strode back towards the door.

As he tapped in the entrance code, she asked, 'Chris, how d'you feel about telling me the little bit you have told me?'

He stood a minute and thought. 'I feel much better,' he said.

'I'm glad that you told me, glad that you felt you could. Chris, did you hear what I said earlier on? I said that…I thought that…'

'You said that you thought you loved me. I don't think that I love you, Joy, I'm absolutely certain of it. I've just realised, and it's a shock. I'm having difficulty coping with the idea.'

'Me, too,' she said shakily.

They parted immediately after that. Joy went home and Chris was able to lose himself in work, the misery of the earlier hours quickly passing. He saw the delivery of two more babies—two tiny pink squalling bundles, two exhausted but radiant mothers' faces. One husband unable to contain his happiness, the other still wondering what was happening to him. This job had its big benefits.

CHAPTER FIVE

CHRIS drove home in the early morning sun. He was to have the rest of the day off, and then start on earlies again two days later. Once again the shift leader had apologised for messing him about, for moving him so rapidly from night shifts to day shifts. But she was short of staff.

'I've got no dependants,' he'd said, 'so I'm glad to do what I can.'

When Chris got home he made himself a light breakfast and sat outside in the sun. Then he worked in his garden for an hour or so, showered and went to bed. He was exhausted.

At five o'clock in the afternoon he got up, made himself a drink and sat out on his patio. For ten minutes he stared out to sea. Then he took out his mobile and phoned Joy.

'I was thinking,' he said. 'You've never been to my home. I'm sitting here in the sun, looking out at the sea, and I'd like you to be with me. Would you like to come to tea?'

'Come to tea? Chris, that's a very old-maidish kind of invitation.' Her voice sounded unusually high. 'How are you? Not still in bed?'

'I'm fine. I've had a little sleep and I'm definitely not an old maid. I've just got up and I'd love to see you.'

'I could come…that is, yes, Chris I want to come to tea with you.' She paused a moment, and then said forlornly, 'But I think I'm a bit frightened.'

'Frightened of me?'

'No, frightened of myself. Or frightened for myself, I don't know. I know I've nearly almost made up my mind about you. But…'

Chris paused before he filled the silence, aware that his invitation had to be just right. Joy was nervous—perhaps she was entitled to be. 'The sun's out on my patio, it's a lovely evening, I'm going to sit and eat outside. I'll cut some fresh salad, I've got some newly baked bread, three different cheeses. Why don't you come and have an alfresco meal with me? We could open a bottle of wine, take things easy, chat like old friends.'

'But we're new friends. We're nearly lovers.'

'Nearly,' he agreed. 'Joy, you think this is something new for you, well, it's new for me, too. You're not the only one who's nervous.'

She giggled. 'Big strong Midwife McAlpine nervous? I just don't believe it. I'll be there in half an hour.'

'Joy, I'll come and fetch you.'

'No!' Her voice was sharp. 'I need to make my own mind up, come on my own. This has all got to be my decision.'

'Then I'll see you soon.' He put down his mobile, opened his palm. It was damp with perspiration.

Chris always kept the cottage neat, that was the way he liked to live. And he had told the absolute truth, that was the meal he was about to have. But he went into the garden and cut three bunches of flowers. One bunch he put on the patio table, the other two he put in his bedroom. The gentle scent spread. Then he went downstairs to prepare the meal.

He waited for Joy by the front window, guessing that knocking on the front door and waiting for him to answer would be a bit of an ordeal. When he saw her car pull up outside he went out to meet her. She was dressed casually again in jeans and long shirt, an outfit much like his own. Her face was wary, and she didn't get out of the car.

'I don't want to park the car in front of your house,' Joy said abruptly. 'Someone from hospital could see it and talk. I don't want that. Well, not yet anyway.'

'That's understandable. If you drive down the side of the house there's space for another car by mine.' He followed her as she drove where he had instructed.

She stepped out of the car, a small overnight bag in her hand. He said nothing, but led her into the garden from the back to the patio, where the meal was set out. Joy looked at him, at the patio doors behind him, at the garden they had just walked through. 'Is this yours? Are you here on your own?'

'I'm renting the house for a year. At the end of that time I have the option to buy if I want. At the moment, I very much want to. This is the first home of my own I've ever had.'

'D'you see to the garden?'

'Well, it was all set up when I arrived. But I'm getting very much to like gardening. I'm learning all about it from a book. I find it restful.' He pulled out a chair. 'D'you want to sit down or would you like a tour of the house?'

She hesitated and then sat. 'I'd like the tour later,' she said. She looked over the garden to the fields and then the sea beyond. 'This is so peaceful, so beautiful. I quite envy you.'

'I'm happy here.' He pulled off the cloth that was covering the table. 'Dinner is already served. I've chilled some white wine for you and I'm going to have some red.' He fetched her bottle from the fridge and poured her a glass.

Joy looked at him suspiciously. 'You're not trying to get me drunk, are you?'

'Certainly not. I'm hoping that you will relax, that's all. I just want us to sit here, eat, drink and chat, and any time that you feel uncomfortable you can go.'

'I don't want to go! I didn't come here just to go away again!'

There was a moment's uneasy silence, and then she sat in the chair he offered her and sighed. She accepted the glass of wine, sipped from it. 'I can hear myself talking,' she said after a while. 'I sound spiky and unfriendly and it's not the way I want to sound. It's not the way I feel. But I'm nervous.'

Chris sat opposite her and poured his own wine. 'I'm nervous, too. But we'll take things easy, see how they progress.' He pushed a bowl across to her. 'Have some salad. I've just mixed the dressing myself.'

She helped herself to salad as he fetched the rolls that were warming in the oven. And after that they both slowly relaxed. She loved the meal he had prepared and they ate and drank slowly as the sun went down, sheltered in the little patio, enjoying each other's company.

They found things to talk about. He told her about his father James, a mining engineer, thinking of retiring but still youthful. Joy told him of her mother Anna, an infant teacher now working on supply, with as many interests now as she'd had when she'd been a young girl. 'I hope I'm like her when I'm her age,' Joy said.

'That's a true compliment. I think the same about my father.'

Then they talked about the hospital management, where they thought the NHS was going. She told Chris she was taking a part-time degree in nursing management. He said he had a degree in midwifery, but was thinking of taking a further degree—a Master of Business Administration—but had put the idea on hold until he was fully established at work.

'After all,' he said slyly, 'I promised to leave after six months if you thought I wasn't up to the job.'

Joy laughed, rather self-consciously. 'I couldn't get rid of you. The rest of the midwives would never forgive me. You're their mascot.'

'They're a good bunch of people to work with. They've made me welcome, I feel I'm one of them. In London people came, you worked with them a while and then they moved on. But here I'm one of a community, and I like it.'

'That's good.' Joy frowned, twisted the stem of her glass nervously. 'Chris, you know when you started, I said some rather unpleasant things about you having been a soldier. Well, I guess I'm sorry I said them. For a start, you've made me realise there's a lot of good in being a soldier, too. And now you're not an ex-soldier to me, you're a midwife and a person I can really trust.'

Chris reached over, covered her hand with his. 'I'm glad you feel you can trust me,' he said.

Shortly afterwards it grew a little chilly, and she insisted on carrying in the dishes and on helping him to wash them. She marvelled at the way the tiny kitchen was laid out, and then insisted on having the tour of the house as the coffee percolated.

It was only a small cottage, the two downstairs rooms knocked through into one. He had bought the minimum of furniture and the apparent bareness of the room was attractive. 'If I do buy the place I'll have a conservatory built over some of the patio, so I can sit out in the garden even in winter,' he told her.

Upstairs Joy saw the spare bedroom neatly made up, the modern bathroom. She peered into his bedroom, registered the double bed and twitched just a little. Chris noticed and gently led her downstairs; the coffee would be ready.

There were only two easy chairs downstairs. Joy sat in one of them and sipped her coffee. 'The house is wonderfully neat, and wonderfully bare,' she said. 'I'm not sure what it tells me about you.'

He shrugged. 'I'm buying things, slowly. When I feel that I really need them. This is the first real home I've ever had of my own. I want things to be just right.'

'I think it's lovely. But this room is very much a man's room. No frills, no pointless knick-knacks. I feel at home here.'

He watched her relax in the chair and stare at him. 'Chris, I brought an overnight bag. If you want me to…I could stay.'

'I want you to stay,' he said softly. 'Joy, do you know how much I want you to stay?'

'I think I do. Chris, it took some courage saying that. I'm still a… Well, I've never… This is a big step for me. I should be nervous, terrified even, and yet it seems as if it's you that's uncertain.' Joy stood, walked over to him, leaned over and kissed him. 'Let's go to bed now. And, Chris, that's the bravest thing that I've ever said.'

He looked up at her, could tell by her rigidity that she meant it. He stood, too, took her in his arms and just held her. 'Everything will be all right,' he said. 'Don't worry, everything will be all right.' Then, when both knew it was the right time, he kissed her. And as they kissed he felt his mounting passion matched by hers.

'I don't know what it is between us,' he murmured, 'but it certainly is something good.'

They walked upstairs, arms clasped round each other's waists. Chris felt her stiffness as they entered his bedroom, so he led her to the window, let her stare out at the fields and the darkening sea. It calmed her a little. Then, again when he thought the time was right, he drew the curtains and switched on the light.

Joy sat on the edge of the bed and smiled up at him. 'You remember when I told you that Henry had complained about you? I said that I didn't approve of short-term relationships and you asked me who had decided that our relationship was going to be short term. I thought that was lovely. I've had odd boyfriends before, of course, but you're the only man I've ever felt I could…well, spend the rest of my life with.'

She didn't notice him tense. 'You're a midwife,' he said quietly. 'You like children. Of course you'll want some of your own.'

'In time,' she said lazily, 'I'd like children—with the right man, of course.'

'With the right man.'

Now she noticed the rigid set of his shoulders, the harshness in his voice. 'Chris, is anything wrong?' she asked.

'Joy, sit on the bed a minute. There's something more I've got to say…do. Remember, you can leave at any time.' He took a great breath, aware of her puzzled eyes studying him.

'I didn't come here to leave.'

'You don't know what I'm going to say.' He folded

his arms, an unconscious gesture showing expected rejection. 'Joy, I can't marry you.'

'No one asked you to!' she said indignantly. 'Chris, that wasn't a proposal, it was just that...I was wondering...' Then she started to think about his words and scrambled to get off his bed. 'You're married! That's it, you're married! Right, I'm off now!'

Chris caught her, eased her back onto the bed. 'No, nothing like that. I'm not, and never have been married. There's no woman waiting for me anywhere. This is something quite different.'

This was something not easy for him, he had never felt the need to explain to a woman before. Previous relationships had never been this intense.

He unbuttoned his shirt, threw it to one side. She had recovered now. 'Aren't you supposed to undress me first?' she asked pertly.

'This is different. Joy, this is hard for me.' He slipped out of his jeans, pushed down the band of his dark blue boxer shorts.

'Joy, you used to be a nurse. I know you worked in A and E for a while. Look at the scars here.'

She slid closer, peering at the well-muscled abdomen. With a finger she traced the scars, the patches of thin whitened skin. There was evidence of surgical incisions. She winced. It must have been an appalling injury. She touched him not as a nurse or a lover but with compassion.

'This was an awful wound,' she said softly. 'What was it?'

'A mortar shell. Lots of shrapnel—little bits of white-hot flying metal tearing through me.' He sat by her on the bed, but stared straight ahead, not looking at her. 'I always wanted children,' he said. 'I think the point of marriage is having children. I looked forward to it some day. Then this injury and things…changed.' He took a deep breath. 'I'm not impotent, Joy. I can enjoy sex, give pleasure, I hope. But one clever bit of flying metal tore through me and cut the vasa deferentia. In effect, gave me a vasectomy. I was told that the chances of my having children are now practically nil. The injury can't be reversed because of the internal scar tissue.'

Joy put her arms round him. 'So you can't have children. You poor man,' she said. 'And I thought you were a big, tough, unfeeling lump.'

'Well, I am,' he said. 'Well, sometimes I am.'

'I think you ought to finish getting undressed and then undress me.'

She kissed him. Her voice was low, her eyes shone. 'I want to love you, Chris. You're the only man I've ever met who I thought I could trust completely. We can worry about children, our future, what's going to happen to us some other time. Now it's just you and me.'

She was right. He thrust the nagging problem of not having children to the back of his mind, he would live for the day. Whatever their future might be, they had now.

Chris switched off the overhead light and switched on the bedside lamp. She was still sitting on the bed, he sat by her. Then he kissed her, gently at first. There was no need to hurry, things had been settled between them. For now, anyway. He kissed her face as she sat, her arms relaxed round him. At first she was still nervous, but then he felt her breathing grow deeper, felt her relaxing. Their kisses grew more languorous, he knew her need for him.

Tentatively he caressed her breasts across the outside

of her shirt, and then with one hand slowly unbuttoned the front. He slipped the shirt from her shoulders, eased it downwards. Her bra was made of pretty white lace. 'I wear sensible underwear to work,' she said, 'but sometimes I think you've got to be exciting…and excited.'

'I'm excited, too,' he said, 'but still I think you're wearing too much.' He reached round her back, deftly undid the bra clip. Then he laid her back on the bed, kissed her shoulders first and then in the deep valley between the slopes of her breasts. Her bra he pulled away, heard her gasp as he teased her with his tongue and then took each stiff peak into his mouth.

She was gorgeous! He leaned over her now, covering her body with his, feeling her warmth, the incredible smoothness of her skin. Softly she sighed, her arms reaching for him, gathering him even closer.

For a while they were secure in the knowledge of each other's body. But then he felt for her jeans, undid the top button and slipped his hand under the waistband of her briefs.

'This is impossible lying down,' she muttered. 'Let me stand up a minute.'

So they both stood and her kissed her standing. It was different. Her breasts were crushed against the muscles of his chest, and he thought he could detect the rapid beating of her heart. Or perhaps it was his heart beating?

Then, to his surprise and delight, Joy took the initiative. Releasing him for a moment, she pushed down briefs and jeans in one movement, then stepped out of the little pool of clothing. Supremely daring, she then did the same for his shorts, and they were standing naked, clasped together.

His arousal was now obvious. He heard her little instinctive intake of breath, felt her move from him, and then surge back again, exciting him more than ever.

When it seemed time Chris reached behind her, pulled back the duvet and lowered her onto the bed. His need for her was now growing irresistibly, but he knew he had to be gentle. He lay by her side, exploring her body, and after a while she did the same for him. Her head was now cradled on his arm, and he could smell the sweetness of her hair, the womanliness of her body.

She felt for his arm, tugged him to tell him to lie on top of her again. He whispered, 'Joy, oh, my Joy.' And she took him into her. Her eyes were closed, there was a small smile on her face. He saw her wince just for a moment but then all was well.

'That feels so good,' she murmured. 'You belong there.'

Together they moved, in a rhythm that both could sense and both could respond to. Both knew that they could wait little longer. There was a formless cry from him, a soft shriek from her as both reached the pinnacle of their passion.

Then they lay side by side, satiated, content.

She whispered, 'I was frightened at first, but that was so good, so right. You are happy, aren't you?'

'I've never been so happy in my life,' he said honestly.

They slept then, her head resting on his arm, his leg over her body.

Chris knew something had been dreadfully wrong, but perhaps it would soon come right. He was panting, terrified, he had to make sense of something. What was it? If he could only know, could only…

'Chris, Chris, it's all right!' From somewhere far distant he heard a voice, anxious but reassuring. 'Chris, it's over now. Try to wake up, everything's all right.'

Where was he? What was he doing? He—

Abruptly, he woke. For a while all he could do was lie there, feel his body covered with sweat, feel the heaving of his chest. But there was the window in front of him, with the curtains he had chosen, the early morning light trying to come through. He was in his own bedroom, the tartan duvet kicked to the foot of the bed. Slowly he regained control, made the fear and horror recede.

He looked to his side. There was Joy, staring at him in dismay. She was sitting up on the bed, one arm holding his shoulder, as if she had been trying to rouse him. Some tiny bit of his mind responded to her beauty, to her naked breasts that he had kissed not so long ago.

'Chris, what is it? All you all right? I've seen people have nightmares before, but never one like that.' Her concern was obvious.

He struggled to sit upright, shook his head to clear it. 'I'm sorry,' he said, 'I really am. It doesn't happen so often now. The doctors said it would pass in time, now perhaps it's only once a month or so. I wouldn't want to scare you, Joy.'

'Well, you did.' She reached over to hug him. 'Why, you're wet through! I'll fetch you a flannel, you'll feel better after a sponge down. Will you be able to sleep?'

Now Chris was fully awake, aware of what had happened and rather embarrassed. No one here knew about his nightmares. He hadn't wanted anyone to know.

'I'm sorry I woke you and, no, I won't be able to sleep. It usually…takes a while.'

'It's morning anyhow. I'm going to fetch you a drink. What would you like?'

'If you're going, I'd like cold milk from the fridge. Here, borrow my dressing-gown.'

Joy wrapped the large garment round her. When she had gone Chris walked to the bathroom and sponged himself down. Then he felt better. What was he going to tell Joy? He guessed she must have been frightened. At times he had frightened himself.

When he got back to the bedroom he found she had opened the curtains, opened the window. He could feel the freshness of the early morning air, hear the early morning birdsong. Beyond was the much-loved vista of fields and the sea. Joy was back in bed, the duvet drawn up round her, her face questioning.

He slipped into bed beside her and she passed him a glass of milk. He saw that she had one herself. 'Just take it easy,' she said. 'I'm in caring nurse mode now, but you frightened me. I'm glad the Chris I know is back.'

'Sorry again,' he said. 'I mean that, I really am sorry.' He sipped his milk.

After a while Joy took his wrist, felt for his pulse. 'You've calmed down now,' she said. 'Do you want to tell me about it? Of course, if you don't, it doesn't matter.' Elaborately casual, she went on, 'You were calling for someone, a woman. Called Matilda. She seemed important to you.'

'She was important. She was a woman I met in Africa.'

'I see,' Joy said, obviously trying not to be judgmental. 'Well, soldiers abroad and…I guess I can understand.'

'I doubt it,' he said wryly. 'I only knew her for a couple of hours and she's dead now.'

'Oh, Chris, I'm sorry! I shouldn't jump to conclusions. Here, I've brought a jug of milk, do you want more?' She took his glass as he tried to get his thoughts in order.

As she leaned over the side table he traced a finger down the line of her back, feeling the warmth, the softness. 'You really are beautiful,' he said. 'That mole on your cheek—it does remind me of Margaret Lockwood. And you have another tiny cluster of moles—here on your breast.' As she turned back with his glass, he stooped to kiss them.

'Drink your milk,' she said, 'then are we going to talk?'

Chris had to make up his mind. 'I'll tell you all about it,' he said, 'and I suppose it'll tell you something about me. But going through it all again can be a bit painful.'

'Then I don't want to—'

'It doesn't matter. I want you to know me, you should know my history.' He drank the rest of the milk in one gulp.

'You already know two bits of the story. First that I tried to help this woman and because of a mistake on my part she and her baby died. Second, that I was blown up by a mortar shell. Now I'm going to fill in the bits in between.'

It wasn't easy starting. He had never told any woman about this. In fact, he had only told David Garner and that had been some years ago. Was Joy really different from anyone he had met in the past six years? Perhaps she was. Whatever, he would take a chance.

'I was leading a four-man patrol through the jungle at night. We were scouting behind enemy lines when we came to a little village which was deserted. God help the poor people there, caught between loyal troops and rebels. When we could help them, it sometimes made the entire exercise worthwhile…'

Now he remembered so well. The heat, the humidity, the constant fear, the need to be on watch all the time. How had he coped? Technically he'd been in charge of the other three men, but they'd worked so well together that there had never been any need to issue orders. That had been the only way to survive.

The village had been deserted. They'd worked their way through it, checking for booby traps. Then he'd heard a moan from one of the huts. He'd held up his hand to stop the ghost-like forms of the men around him.

Was it a trap? He crept to the door, kicked it open, leaped inside, finger on the trigger of his sub-machine gun. There was a scream of pain and terror.

Quickly he flicked the torch on and off, then softly called to his men to continue the search. There was no danger here. A few sticks of rough furniture, a cold cooking stove, a bare mud floor. In one corner was a bed, covered in rags, and on the bed was a woman. She was in labour. The rest of the village had fled, but she couldn't move.

He had quite a detailed knowledge of first aid, and a very good first-aid kit. But the kit was for dealing with trauma—for bullet wounds, for shrapnel splinters—not for delivering a baby. He'd had no training at all in this, it wasn't a front-line occurrence.

He knew he should walk out of the hut, this wasn't his problem. But out of sheer humanity he couldn't.

One of the other three carried a radio set. Chris went to fetch it and called up his HQ. He guessed what the

first reaction would be and he was right. 'You're a soldier, McAlpine, not a ruddy midwife. Get on with the
patrol!'

'We're supposed to look after these people, not leave
them to die. Now, I know there's a medical officer
there—put him on the radio,' Chris snapped back. 'And
I don't want an orderly—I want a doctor.'

He was in luck, there was a doctor there. He was
further in luck, the doctor was sympathetic. And so, step
by step, illuminated simply by a torch, following instructions over a crackling radio, Chris tried to be a
midwife for the first time.

'I found myself getting really into it, even enjoying
it,' he told Joy. 'I felt I was doing something…more
constructive than I had done before. But there were
problems—I thought the baby should be born—poor
Matilda was in agony, something was wrong. It was hell
trying to follow the doctor's instructions, but eventually
we decided that it was a shoulder distochia.'

Joy looked at him in horror. 'You'd never delivered
a baby before—and you had a shoulder distochia.' This
was a rare condition when the baby's shoulders could
not pass the pelvic inlet. 'What did you do?'

'All I wanted to do was get away from there. But I
couldn't leave Matilda. Over the radio the doctor told
me how to put her in the McRobert position, with her
thighs on her abdomen, and I performed my first episiotomy. Then it was a case of trying to ease the baby
out by hand.'

He could feel the tightness of Joy's grip. Without him
noticing, she had seized his hand.

He had thought he'd been doing well. There had been
some movement of the baby, and he'd thought perhaps,
just perhaps, he might succeed. Then the radio had

crackled again. Intelligence had said that rebels were moving back towards the village, they were to get out at once.

'We always carried a stretcher, Joy. We could have carried Matilda through the jungle for a couple of hours then there was a lorry waiting for us. But I didn't want to move her—Matilda wouldn't have survived it and the baby would certainly be dead. So I told my men to retreat and said that I'd stay for another few minutes, it should be enough time to deliver the baby. They didn't want to leave me behind, I had to pull rank on them.'

The rest of the story was quickly told. The rebels hadn't reoccupied the village—they'd shelled it with a mortar. He remembered hearing the thumps of the first two explosions, then there had been the scream of another shell and he'd known it was going to be close. It was close. And even now the terror of that moment came back to him.

'It tore through the roof of Matilda's hut and exploded inside. She and the baby were killed. Just another statistic. I was…lucky. I woke up on the stretcher. My men had heard the shelling, disobeyed orders themselves and come back for me.'

For the first time Chris turned to look at Joy. He could still feel the tightness of her grip, but now he saw her shoulders shaking, knew that she was sobbing.

'Hey, it was all a long time ago,' he said. 'Since then I've moved on. There are things you have to forget.'

'*You* haven't forgotten,' she wept, 'so don't tell me to forget either. Come on, tell me the rest of the story.'

He shrugged. 'My promising military career was over. I'd been injured too badly. My disobeying orders was quietly overlooked and I was invalided out. Anyway, I decided to train as a midwife. I already knew

David Garner—I had a talk with him, he suggested it. You know he was in the army before he decided to specialise in O and G?'

'Yes, I know. Chris, why d'you blame yourself for the death of that woman? You do, don't you? But it wasn't your fault. You made a good decision—you did what you thought was right at the time.'

'I know I shouldn't blame myself,' he said, 'but I do. It's the army way. If you take a decision, you live with the consequences. Maybe I should have tried to move her. I'll never know.'

'And you still have the nightmares?'

'They were much more common,' he said, 'now they're quite rare. And in time the doctors said they'll disappear.'

'D'you think that talking about what happened might help? You've kept it bottled up for too long.'

Chris looked at her, puzzled. 'D'you know,' he said, 'that's an interesting thought. But now I'm tired of talking of the past.'

'It's early morning,' she said, 'and I feel wide awake. What can we do now?'

'I can think of one thing,' he said, and pushed her back down on the bed.

Later he cooked her breakfast and they had a leisurely meal on the patio. 'Are we going to spend the rest of the day together?' he asked.

She shook her head, 'I'd love to but no. I've things I just have to do at home, as I'm driving down to London tomorrow. I'm afraid I'll be staying for a few days, it's part of the course I'm on.'

'Will you miss me?'

'Of course I'll miss you! I've just found you—we've

found each other—every minute I'm away from you is wasted. Chris, I'm in love with you! I want to…give you so much. And I think that last night was the best night of my life.'

'That's lovely. I think the same myself.'

'I shall come to stay again,' she said, 'that is, if I'm invited.'

'You're invited at any time,' he said.

CHAPTER SIX

IT WAS part of Joy's management system that none of the midwives stayed in one particular section of the unit. They were to be moved so that they had experience of all the different kinds of work. Chris liked the delivery suite best, but was quite willing to take his turn in the day clinic, which was held in another part of the hospital, or the ante- or postnatal wards, or even in Theatre. He knew the wider experience would turn him into a better midwife.

Today he was assisting David Garner in Theatre with a couple of Caesarean sections. Two midwives would be present, one helping David as scrub nurse, handing him the instruments, the other—Chris—taking the baby when it was born. There would be a paediatrician to examine, perhaps to take charge of the newborn baby, but if there were no problems, the baby would be the responsibility of the midwife.

Both births were simple, straightforward. After taking the first baby, Chris performed the full baby check, slipped on the ID bands, snapped on a cord clamp and trimmed the cord. When the mother was ready to be transferred to the recovery room, Chris slid the baby in beside her. Mother and baby were together for the first time. Usually the mother was still groggy from the anaesthetic. But Chris loved to watch her eyes flick open, to focus somehow on the little white-wrapped bundle.

It was after the second birth. Chris was in the recovery room, writing up his baby notes. The mother had smiled at her child and gone back to sleep.

But this particular baby wasn't going to sleep. For five minutes now he had cried, a tremendously powerful cry from a pair of lungs so tiny. So Chris picked him up, held him close to his chest and face and rocked him. And the baby stopped crying.

Then, to his surprise, Joy came into the recovery room. She glanced at the sleeping mother then looked at the tall figure still in theatre greens, holding the baby so confidently.

'That would make a nice but an unusual picture,' she said. 'Male midwife and child.'

Chris rocked his little charge again. 'It's one of the perks of the job.'

'Yes, I know. Let me see.' She peered at the now contented little face. 'Do you ever wonder who—or what—you're bringing into the world, Chris?'

'Sometimes. I know that this production-line method of having babies is most efficient—but sometimes I wonder what it would be like to look after a mother right from when she first needs antenatal care through to well after birth.'

'Like it used to be,' Joy said. 'It was the way I trained, I much preferred it. But these days only the father can do that.' Then she realised what she had said and winced. 'Chris, I'm so sorry! After what you told me that was insensitive, it was a terrible thing to say!'

'It doesn't matter, it's something I've got used to,' he said softly. 'But what are you doing here? I thought you were off to London.'

'I am. But I heard you were in here, so I came—to see you and to say I'll miss you.' She smiled mischie-

vously. 'And I'm still your boss, you know. I came in
here to see how well you're coping.'

'And have I passed?'

'Oh, yes,' she said, 'you've passed every test now.
D'you think you could ease that baby to one side a
minute, and kiss me?'

Two hours later Chris found himself drinking coffee
with David. Unusually, there was nothing requiring
their immediate attention. A rare chance to relax.

'You seem pleased with life,' David said with a broad
smile. 'The job working out to your satisfaction?'

'Perfectly. I love it up here, I'm happy in my cottage,
happy in my work. How are you doing?'

David shrugged. 'I've got the usual clinical problems.
I know babies don't come along just at a time to suit
me, but I can live with that. It's what I'm paid for, what
I'm good at. I enjoy it. But I seem to spend most of my
time arguing with hospital managers at the moment. I'm
more interested in saving babies than saving money.
You've heard about our financial problems?'

'I've heard about them,' Chris said, 'but so far I've
remained well away from them.' He glanced out of the
window. 'Another glorious day, David. Why don't you
play truant tonight and come for a walk with me along
the cliffs? We could finish off with a pint and a pub
meal. Stay the night if you like. There's a couple of
things I'd like to talk to you about.'

'Chris, I'd love to but I just couldn't spare the—yes,
I could! I'll phone Mary. She'll be pleased to hear I'm
out with you. And I'll bet she asks if you are involved
with anyone at the moment—she wants to see you
settled.'

'Well,' said Chris, 'perhaps you can say that I am—sort of.'

David frowned. 'I think I can guess who you mean. Is this what we're going to talk about?'

'Your advice has always been good in the past,' said Chris.

It was good to walk with an old friend. The two men paced along the cliff path, admiring the view and reminiscing about old times. Then David suddenly said, 'Now, tell me about you and Joy Taylor. Let me say first of all that I know at times she appears a bit withdrawn. But she's very good at her work, a caring person, and she deserves the best.'

'You're sure I want to talk about Joy?' Chris asked with a smile.

'I'm not a fool. I can see, I can feel what's happening between you. Chris, I don't want her hurt.'

'I don't want her hurt either. Whatever it is between us, it's very real. A lot of the time she used to say that she didn't like me, that I had a military mind. But we've got over that now.'

'So what's wrong?' asked David. 'I can tell you've got something on your mind.'

'I love her,' Chris said flatly. 'She's a wonderful woman, she should have children and she can't have them with me. I feel sorry for myself but I'm not going to make her sacrifice her chances of happiness by marrying me.'

David looked doubtful. 'I didn't know you were thinking of marriage, Chris.'

'I'm not. I want to but I'm not. I'm just worried that things might inevitably move that way. She deserves a family of her own. And I have told her that I can't have children.'

'That was honest. But, then, you always were a fair man. What did she say?'

'Said we didn't need to worry about it yet. That we had today and that was enough for now. But she'll change her mind, in time we'll have to talk.'

'True.' They walked in silence a little further. Then David said, 'If it got that far you could always adopt children.'

'We could. Sometimes it's a great idea. But maybe she wants children of her own. We both know that look a woman gives when she first sees her newborn baby. Well, Joy is entitled to look that way.'

'So what are you going to do?' This was the question he had to answer.

The path they were following had dropped from the clifftop nearly to the beach, and now they were making their way steeply upwards, walking in single file through thickets of brambles. For a while conversation was difficult, and Chris had time to think. But then they reached the clifftop again, and by mutual consent sat on a convenient rock.

'For a start, we might not be as suited as we first thought. Only time, the next few weeks, will tell that. But I've never been more attracted to a woman, and I think she feels the same. I could say that I've told her my situation, she knows we can't have children, now she must make up her own mind. But that's just not fair. It's up to me to make the break. But, David...she means so much to me.'

'You've got a problem,' David said moodily.

After a while he went on, 'I know you'll do the right thing, even if it is hard. But remember, she is also entitled to make decisions about her own life, you have to give her that chance. If she wants to stay by you, then you'll have to let her.'

'I don't know whether to be pleased or sorry at that,' said Chris.

'The midwives elected you to be their representative while I was away?' Joy asked, as if she could hardly believe the news.

'Elected me unanimously,' said Chris blandly. 'This could be a recognition of my obvious abilities. Or it could be that none of them wanted the job.'

They eyed each other thoughtfully. This was a new development in their relationship. Something entirely different. They were in her office, both for once not in uniform. Both were wearing dark suits. The meeting to come was going to be a formal one.

'D'you understand what's happening?' she asked. 'D'you know the background?'

'I don't know the details and I think the details are all-important. I want to see figures, exact facts, not have to listen to rumours and idle gossip.' He knew his voice was curt, but he also knew that what had happened wasn't her fault. So he tried to relax, appear more friendly. 'I'm sure there'll be no disagreements between us two.'

'Well, no professional disagreements,' Joy said. 'Basically, the hospital trust is short of money. Every department has to economise somehow. I think that the idea in the background is that we close a ward, have fewer beds, perhaps have compulsory redundancies.'

'I thought as much. I also thought that having an elected representative such as myself at the meeting might be a way of making redundancies more accept-able to the staff.'

'That crossed my mind,' she admitted. 'Incidentally, David Garner is absolutely on our side. It's senior man-agement we have to fight.'

'I could have guessed that.' Chris glanced at his watch. 'Shall we go?'

As they walked across the hospital grounds he said cheerfully, 'Fortunately everyone knows we're heading for a meeting. They won't think that anything's going on between us.'

'They will in time if we keep on seeing each other,' she said gloomily. 'Hospitals always gossip.'

'I can stand it if you can,' he said urbanely.

They entered the main building, went up the impos-ing steps to the big committee room on the first floor. There were perhaps thirty people there, sitting round a long polished table and chatting idly. In front of each was a small card with name, rank and occupation. Chris and Joy found their places together at the bottom of the table. They waved at David Garner, who was near the top.

'All these important people,' she whispered to Chris. 'Don't you feel overwhelmed?'

'In negotiations, face is as important as facts,' he whispered back, 'so look confident. Always keep calm and don't show what you want until the last possible minute. This is a battle. We have to fight it with brains.'

'This isn't a battlefield! It's a hospital!'

'This is a place where people are trying to get their own way. They're prepared to make sacrifices in order to gain advantages. And that in essence is what a battle is. Now, don't get mad and don't start insisting at once on what you must have.'

'Hey, I'm not really mad. And who's senior here?' It was said with a smile.

'You're the better midwife. But I've done more fighting than you—and negotiating. Now, we're starting.'

The hospital Chief Executive Officer had entered the chamber, and started by handing everyone a sheaf of papers. 'Ladies and gentlemen, thank you for coming. I'll be blunt. For various reasons we are short of cash, and we shall have to retrench. On your behalf I have written to the press, to our local MPs, to the Secretary of State for Health. I have even written to the Lottery. I am still writing, and perhaps in time things may improve. But now we have to do something. I have spoken to all departmental heads, and all have said that they cannot cut any more. I sympathise with that, but cuts must be made, and I have drawn up a possible plan...'

After that the meeting followed a predictable path. Everyone was angry, everyone thought that another department wasn't doing enough. Chris had guessed this would happen, and said little even when Joy joined the argument, outraged at the cuts suggested for her own department. She nudged him, irritated. 'Have you nothing to say?'

'Not yet,' he said. He carried on studying the papers in front of him, at long last in possession of the facts he needed.

The O and G Department was under attack from Alfred Comber, the senior paediatrician of the hospital, a bombastic man who had been a consultant for many years. He was genuinely upset, he said, but he believed that O and G should be cut, Paediatrics should not. The O and G department would have to lose staff. What made things worse was that just as the argument started a secretary came in with a message. David Garner had to leave at once. Alfred Comber was getting the support he needed.

Finally, Chris decided it was time for him to speak. 'It's good to see Mr Comber is on our side. I've been looking though the details provided, and I believe that if we rescheduled the patterns of work of nurses, midwives, ancillary staff and doctors, we could manage without having to sack anyone.'

'Sorry,' said the CEO. 'I've tried that, it's just not possible.'

'I believe it is possible,' said Chris. 'This rescheduling would, of course, have to include the most senior posts in the departments. And I know that my own consultant, Mr Garner, would be quite happy to work to a different pattern.'

'Quite impossible,' boomed Mr Comber. 'I cannot possibly alter my work patterns.'

'It might come to a choice between being paid for seeing some private patients or agreeing to hospital staff being sacked,' said Chris. 'Which would you prefer?'

All round the table were suddenly silent. No one talked to Alfred Comber like that!

Mr Comber's already high-coloured face turned almost purple. 'I should...I should like to see these so-called reschedulings,' he said, 'though I doubt I'll pay much attention to them. The Staff will have to be retrenched and it's no concern of mine! I'm not being told what to do by a...by a male midwife!'

Chris smiled, and suddenly Mr Comber decided to keep quiet. Calmly Chris said, 'I am here to represent the interests of the midwives and then the hospital as a whole. I heard no talk of confidentiality here. It would make a great quote in the Northern papers—''Staff will have to be sacked and it's no concern of mine''.'

Mr Comber couldn't believe this. No one had ever spoken to him like this before. 'You wouldn't dare,' he yelled. 'If you want any kind of career in this hospital…'

'And then threatened the career of a junior member of staff,' Chris went on. 'Mr Comber, let me tell you one certain thing. Yes, I would dare.'

The appalled CEO now decided he had better speak. 'Gentlemen, gentlemen,' he said, 'perhaps we should speak with a little more…a little less passion. I am sure that both Mr Comber and Mr McAlpine have the best interests of the hospital at heart. Perhaps if Mr McAlpine could forward his suggestions to me—say in a fortnight's time—we could study the proposals.'

There was a general mumbled agreement, and Mr Comber rose and crashed out of the door.

'Good meeting,' Chris said to Joy.

'You did that on purpose didn't you?' Joy asked as they walked back towards the O and G department. 'You deliberately provoked that man so he would make a fool of himself.'

They had decided not to stay for coffee after the meeting. But three or four people had said that they were interested in what Chris had said, that perhaps it was a way forward—if everyone would agree.

Chris didn't answer for a minute, but then he said, 'Perhaps, as a result of what I said, we might not have to lose a couple of midwives. That means more mums and more babies get better care. Isn't that a good thing?'

'It's a super thing. You did more good at that meeting than I did. But how you did it…' Joy shook her head. 'At first I thought you were a bit overawed by the people there. But you weren't. You were ruthless. And they're not used to people like you.'

'People like me,' he said reflectively. 'Aren't I a good midwife, Joy?'

'You know you're an excellent midwife. And I know that you're a kind and a loving and a giving person. It's just that at times you show—well, it's not exactly a hard streak, it's just that you sometimes get what you want by ways that seem a bit…unusual.'

'Like taking my boss to dinner at Croston's?'

'A very unusual thing to do.' They were walking through the grounds now, trees hiding them from public view. She stopped, reached up and kissed him quickly. 'You might have saved me from having to decide which midwife I had to let go. And I love you for it, and I don't care how you do it.'

'I'll be good. Can I have another kiss?'

'No. We can be seen now.' They paced on in contented silence.

'I'll write a report about what we've just decided and I'll be calling a meeting to talk to the other midwives,' he said. 'Will you be there?'

'I'll be there. What are you going to say?'

'Well, nothing about threats or headlines. And no raising hopes either. Just that there might be a chance for us to avoid compulsory redundancies.'

'I'll bet you get what you want,' she said.

They had the meeting the next day. Chris spoke briefly but eloquently. At the end of it all the midwives agreed that they would support him in his proposals to alter the work schedules if it would mean that none of them were sacked.

'You gave them just what they wanted to hear,' Joy

told him afterwards, 'but you were fair about everything. You didn't give them false hope but morale is
higher than it has been in weeks. There's something
about you—you inspire confidence. You even make me
feel confident, and sometimes I'm an old cynic about
hospital politics.'

'I want you to feel more than confidence in me,' he
said.

Two days later, things were different.

'You've been violent again, Mr McAlpine,' Joy said,
'and uttering threats, too. This time against a member
of the hospital staff.'

Chris smiled, stretched his arms over his head. 'It's
called the red mist, ma'am. Comes over me every now
and again. When it does I just have to hurt and maim
and kill. But it's only about once every two months.'

'Hmm,' said Joy. They were in her office and she
had just sent for him. 'This is a bit serious, Chris. I'm
not sure what to do. I'm also not sure I should be asking
you.'

'Perhaps you're right,' he agreed. 'Do I gather young
Carole Green has been in to see you?'

'She has. She didn't exactly make a formal complaint—rather she asked my advice—but she said that
you suggested very strongly that she ought to see me.'

Chris nodded, serious now. 'I'll tell you my version
of the story, then it's your decision what to do about it.
I was working lates last night and there weren't a lot
of people around at midnight. There was no light in that
waiting room that the patients use, but I thought I heard
a noise. So I went in and there was Henry Trust looking
angry and Carole looking frightened to death. When I

walked in Henry let go of her. You can guess what he'd been trying. Did she show you her arm?'

'No,' Joy said.

'Have a look, it'll be bruised. Anyway, when I walked in, Carole ran for it and Henry got angry and asked me what I thought I was doing. I said I was looking after the welfare of a junior member of staff. He said, ''We all know how you look after the welfare of the females here.'' So I walked up to him and said the last man I saw molesting female staff needed a stay in hospital—did he remember?'

'You didn't touch him?'

Chris looked astounded. 'Certainly not! We're all professionals here. I just walked up to him. He had his back to the wall.'

'How close to him did you get?'

Chris pondered. 'Our noses were about half an inch apart,' he admitted. 'Henry looked a little…unnerved.'

Joy managed to suppress a giggle. 'That I can imagine,' she said.

'Anyway, afterwards I went to find Carole and told her that if she felt she was being subjected to unreasonable behaviour she should report it to you. Carole said that at one time you were supposed to be fond of Henry. I said even if you were married to him, you'd see that she was treated fairly.'

'Hmm. That was good of you. Was it a serious assault, d'you think?'

'That's up to Carole to say. But I think not. Largely because I don't think Henry has the guts for a serious assault.'

'You've got a gentle way of saying things, haven't you? All right, I'll have another word with Carole, look at her arm and then have a word with David Garner. Ask him to speak to Henry unofficially.'

'Best way,' Chris agreed. 'Wait until Carole tells you exactly what happened. I'd better get back to work.'

Joy stood and walked to her bookcase, which he had to pass to get to the door. '*How* close were you to Henry?' she asked.

'This close.' He put his arms round her, touched her nose with his.

'No wonder he was…affected,' said Joy. 'I think it's happening to me too but in a different way.'

He bent to kiss her. Her telephone rang. 'Saved by the bell,' she said.

It was Friday night, late, and Chris was more irritated, more impatient than he had thought possible. He felt like a child waiting for Christmas! He stood, pulled back his curtains again. No sign of anyone arriving.

Joy had had work to do, a meeting to attend. She had phoned telling him that she couldn't get there for the meal he had invited her to, and would have sandwiches at the meeting. But she would bring a bottle of wine. 'I'm so looking forward to seeing you,' she'd said.

His attention strayed at the vital moment. He picked up a book and then there was a hesitant rap on his door.

Chris tried to kiss her, but she turned her head so he could only kiss her cheek. 'I need to calm down,' she said. 'I'm still wound up from that meeting. But I'm so glad to be here, and so glad to see you.'

'I'm glad to see you, too,' he said. He looked at her. Joy wore her dark formal suit, had an overnight bag in one hand and a bottle of champagne in the other, and looked absolutely delightful.

'We've got to talk and I want to talk in comfort. In

fact, I want to talk in bed. May I have a bath first? I'd like to wash the smell of the hospital off me.'

'Have what you want,' he said. 'Shall I come and wash your back?'

She considered. 'I think not. It might lead to…things. Chris, let me go upstairs for a while. I know it's your bedroom but I want to make it a bit my own.'

'Whatever you want,' he said. 'You know the way.'

Now he knew she was here, in his house, he knew he could wait. There was an intimacy in feeling her presence upstairs, in hearing doors shut, the odd bump. Soon they would be together. Waiting was a sharp pleasure. He went to his kitchen.

After half an hour she called him. 'You can come up now—bring the wine. And what's that wonderful smell?'.

Chris took the tray from the oven, arranged the contents on a plate. 'Little things,' he said as he walked upstairs. 'I read this article on how to impress a woman, and it said cook her tiny titbits and gave a few recipes. So here's what I've done.'

Then he blinked as he entered his bedroom. The lights were turned off, she had lit the room with candles. On his dressing-table stood a bowl full of water and small glass balls, a light in the centre reflecting shimmering patterns on his walls. Joy was sitting on the bed in a long satin gown, and he thought that, in the flickering half-light, he had never seen her so lovely.

'Sit here by me,' she said, 'and tell me what's on that tray in your hand.'

He showed her what he had made—tiny salmon tartlets, asparagus on rye toast, duck pâté on biscuits, a variety of things. 'They're all wonderful! I wasn't hungry before, but now…'

So they ate together. Only a few mouthfuls, but satisfying. And afterwards he popped the cork of the champagne and filled two flutes.

After they had finished the first glass Chris sat on the bed by her, put his arm round her. She pulled the arm against her cheek, rubbed it there and then moved it away. 'I told you that I needed to talk to you,' she said, 'and when I go over things it tends to upset me. But I've got to tell you.'

'If it's going to upset you why can't it wait? We've got tomorrow.'

'No, it has to be now! But you can hold me a bit. You sit at the top of the bed and I'll sit between your legs.' She leaned back against him, her head against his chest, and held his arms in her hands.

'You know I used to be against what I thought was your military mind—the way you seemed to cut straight through troubles, did what had to be done no matter what the consequences?'

'I know what you mean.'

'Well, I know better now. But it was to do with my father. I thought you were like him. I told you, he was in the navy, a lieutenant commander. He died eight years ago when I was twenty. A pointless accident, a car crash at a naval base.'

Joy stopped talking, but he said nothing. He felt that this was a story she had to tell in her own way, in her own time.

'I—we—didn't see much of him. He was away at sea a lot. Perhaps he found it hard to settle to family life. We were never a...close family. He was very happy when I started to train as a nurse. It was the kind of thing he thought women should do. Sometimes I wonder if he quite knew what to do with a daughter. I suppose he loved me, but it was in his own way.'

'You can only love in your own way,' Chris said gently.

'Yes, well, it didn't do me much good.'

Her back was pressed against his chest, he could feel her body with her arms. And he knew this was upsetting her. Her breathing was faster and at times she wriggled uneasily against him.

'I had a brother called Tim, he was one year older than me and we were very close. We were friends rather than brother and sister. Dad was very proud of Tim. He did well at school, joined the school cadet force and did well there, too. And at the end of his time at school Tim was offered a commission in the navy. Of course, Dad was over the moon. But Tim said he wanted a year off—three of his pals were going to South America for a year to join a camp doing some construction work and some teaching little kids. Tim wanted to go with them.'

'And your father didn't think it a good idea?'

'That's an understatement. He raged and screamed and just wouldn't have it. The other problem was that just at that time my mother found a growth in her breast. It turned out to be benign, but we didn't know that. We felt we had to keep family rows away from her. Anyway, reluctantly Tim joined the navy. And he kept getting letters from his pals, saying what a good time they were having. I saw the letters.'

'Did he enjoy his time in the navy?' Chris asked.

'Who can tell? He didn't say much about his feelings after that, he was taught not to talk about emotional things. You know that, don't you?'

'I can sympathise,' Chris admitted.

'Anyway…' He felt Joy draw a breath, felt her body

go rigid, her hands tighten on his arms. 'He was killed. Not even in a real war, some kind of exercise that went wrong. We never got the full details. His life was spoiled, wasted, going out to South America—the only thing he really ever wanted to do—denied him. The navy sent a man to talk to us, and he talked about him being a hero, serving his country. He didn't know Tim! I said Tim had been too young to serve his country. And now in you I can see bits of my father and bits of what Tim turned into. The things that killed him. And that's why I thought I couldn't love you, but I do!'

Now she was weeping, her body racked with sobs. As he pulled her to him he could feel the warmth of her tears on his chest. All he could do was hold her. He knew there was nothing he could say.

So he held her. She said nothing and in time he could feel her breathing deepen, feel her heartbeat slow. Her grip on him slackened and he knew she was asleep.

Chris looked round his bedroom. Two of the candles were guttering, their flames flickering. Gently he laid Joy down, pulled the duvet over her. Then he blew out the rest of the candles, undressed and stretched himself beside her.

She felt warm next to him. In the room there was the not unpleasant smell of hot wax. It contrasted with the scent of the womanliness of her. Chris sighed and closed his eyes. But it was some time before he slept.

CHAPTER SEVEN

THE morning was different. Joy's misery of the night before had vanished—perhaps telling Chris about Tim had somehow helped her. But she woke before him. He felt her hair stroking his face and then the softest of kisses on his cheek.

'I am awake,' he mumbled.

'Then go back to sleep. Last night you looked after me. Now I want to do something for you. No!' she said as he started to sit up. 'I said stay asleep. I'll be back soon.' She slipped out of bed.

Chris couldn't sleep but he lay there in a happy, drowsy state, knowing that this morning things would be better. And from below came the scent of freshly made coffee.

He looked at his ceiling and frowned, puzzled. It was another fine day. There was a shaft of early morning sunlight across the room, but also a light dancing round it. Sometimes the light was coloured, sometimes just a pinpoint of brightness. He watched it, entranced. What was it? He sat up.

Hanging from his curtain rail, in the gap in the curtains, was a crystal. One of the windows was open and the crystal moved and twisted in the slight breeze, making the prisms reflect colours all round his room.

Joy came in, holding a tray with two giant mugs of coffee. 'Did you put that crystal there?' Chris asked.

'Yes. They're supposed to bring good luck. I don't

think that they do, but I like the way the light flashes everywhere. Doesn't it make your bedroom lovely?'

'Not as much as you do,' he said. 'But, yes, it makes my bedroom lovely.'

She sat in bed next to him and they drank their coffee. Now they knew each other a little better and were content in each other's company, there was no desperate urge to seize what they could before the chance perhaps disappeared. They could experiment, take time to stroke and touch and kiss. Two bodies, each with so much to offer. And later, after the inevitable but much-postponed climax, there was a deeper happiness and contentment.

They lay side by side, letting the coolness of the breeze play over their heated bodies, watching the light of the crystal dance round them.

'I've just looked at the schedules, I see you've got a couple of days off in the middle of the week,' Joy said drowsily, her head nestled into his shoulder. 'What are you going to do with them?'

He paused before saying, 'I've got a bit of unfinished business in London I'm afraid. Military stuff. I'm sorry about it.'

'You should be, I was going to ask if I could come round. Can you tell me what you're doing?'

Again there was a short pause. Chris shrugged. 'Just stuff. If I can, I'll tell you when I get back.'

'I can wait.' She rubbed her head up and down his neck. 'Being here is lovely, Chris. Just lying here, having you by my side, knowing you'll always be with me.'

He didn't want to break the mood, to spoil the happiness they were both sharing. But there was something he had to say. It was against his nature to remain silent, to refuse to face up to a challenge. Joy had chosen to ignore what he had told her—that he couldn't have children. But he couldn't ignore it.

'Always is a long time Joy,' he said. 'We don't know what time will bring.'

She twisted her head to peer at him. 'That's not a very nice thing to say, Chris. I want to be contented and happy and with you.'

'That's what I want. But I can't forget. You'll want children—you're a woman born to have them. And you can't have them with me.'

'It doesn't matter. We've got each other for now, and we'll let the future take care of itself. We're both too young to worry.'

It was what he needed to hear. But he wondered if he could hear the faintest touch of uncertainty in her voice. He desperately hoped not.

In fact, it was a while before they could meet again properly. They had passed in the corridor, smiling politely. Once or twice Chris had been into her room to steal a kiss. But mostly they had been apart. Joy still wanted their affair kept quiet, though she knew that in time it would come out. 'We'll both get talked about, Chris. Let's leave it until it's absolutely necessary.'

He had phoned her as soon as he'd returned from London, asking her to come round early in the evening. 'Something special, Chris? You've got a surprise for me?'

'I think so,' he'd said heavily. 'See you at seven, then?' And he had rung off.

Joy arrived promptly at seven. 'I brought my overnight bag,' she said, waving it. 'I hoped I might be invited to stay the night. But I'm not going to force myself on you.'

He smiled weakly. 'You're always more than welcome to stay. I hope you still want to after you hear
what I've got to say.'

That shook her. She looked at him apprehensively,
glanced round the living room where she'd been so
happy. 'I don't like the sound of that,' she said. 'You're
going to tell me something...more about yourself?'

'Not about me. Sit down, Joy. This won't take long
and then—I hope—we can be like we were before. I
don't like taking chances, but this is one.'

Now she was really alarmed. 'Come on, Chris, tell
me!'

He led her to a comfortable chair, sat facing her. On
her right was a small table with a telephone on it, and
by the telephone a number written on a piece of paper.
From a cupboard he took two glasses and a decanter,
poured them both a brandy.

'You know I went to London. Well, I still have quite
a few military contacts there so I also did some re-
search. Now there's something you've got to do yourself.' Chris pointed to the telephone. 'That's the number
of Chief Petty Officer Peter Lambert. He was with your
brother when he was killed. He saw a lot of him in the
last few days of his life. He'll tell you how your brother
died. I think it might be good for you to speak to him.'

Joy stared at him, seemingly unable to speak. Then,
eventually, she gasped, 'Why...why did you do this?
I'm hurting already. I'm trying to live with the hurt and
you're making it worse. Why do you have to bring it
up? Chris, this is too cruel of you!'

His face paled. 'You said it. You're hurting already,
and part of it is because you just don't know. Talking
to Lambert might put some of that hurt right. It's always
best to know, Joy.'

Chris stood. 'Lambert will be waiting by the phone for the next two hours. We agreed that. Now it's up to you whether you want to phone or not.'

She remained there, as still as if frozen. He saw two tears appear and trickle unheeded down her cheeks. The silence between them seemed to stretch on without limits. He would not speak first. This she had to decide for herself.

Eventually she said, her voice quavering, 'I think I want to…but I can't, I daren't… Chris, will you phone for me?'

He mustn't show the pain it cost him to answer. To refuse her hurt more than anything he had ever felt. But he knew what his answer had to be.

'No, Joy, I won't phone for you. This is something you must do on your own. Take a mouthful of brandy and reach for that phone. I'll be waiting outside.'

Chris took his glass and walked to the patio door. Once outside he pressed the door shut, hearing the swish of the rollers, the thunk of it closing. He had one last sight of Joy sitting perfectly still. Then he turned his back on her.

For the longest half hour he could remember he sat on his patio, oblivious of the beauty of the evening, the smells of the countryside, the distant sighing of the sea. Then the patio door opened and Joy came out. In her hands were two mugs of tea. Prosaically, she said, 'I made myself at home in your kitchen. Got us a cup of tea each.'

'I'm glad you can feel at home here.' She sat opposite him and he asked cautiously, 'Did you phone?'

'Yes, I phoned. I liked Peter Lambert. I'm going to write to him to say thank you.'

'So you're glad you're phoned?'

She reflected. He could see her eyes were red, she had been weeping. 'I suppose I'm glad,' she said. 'I know I'll be more glad in the morning. Talking to Peter brought a lot back. He told me things about my brother that I remembered, that made it hard for me. But…Peter said Tim was very happy in his work, he'd got to like it. And he was good at his job. And last of all, he was a hero. He died helping someone.' Now the tears started again.

After a while Joy shook herself, took out a handkerchief and wiped her face. 'There's something else, though,' she said, her voice now stronger. 'One thing more. You took an awful chance looking up this man and then telling me to phone him. You could have spoiled all that we have, all this new relationship. I still feel a bit, well, manipulated. You've been making decisions that perhaps I ought to have made.'

'I did take a chance,' Chris agreed gravely. 'But I wanted to make you happier. If things need doing they should be done. And was I successful?'

'Yes,' she said. 'You were successful.'

'So how're you getting on with Joy?' David asked as they relaxed some time later. 'Mary was asking. When I told her you have a partner she was excited. She really wants to get you married off.'

'Joy and I are doing fine,' Chris said. 'We're getting somewhere and I don't think I've ever been happier. You know she's been off for the last three weeks on this course in London? And just when things were going well for us.'

'Do you keep in touch?'

'Of course we do. She phones me two or three times a week and we have a long chat.'

'So how d'you talk when she does ring you?'

Chris shrugged. 'Sometimes it's difficult. Neither of us much likes phoning, we both find it hard to say how we feel into a little bit of plastic. When we're together we manage wonderfully, if we can see and touch each other then there's nothing finer. But over the phone we both need time to relax. We're learning about each other.'

'Learning about each other should be fun. It takes time, you don't want to hurry too much.'

'I'm learning that. The first time I saw her it was…fantastic. But I suppose it was basically physical. Now, the more I see her, the more I like her. No, the more I love her!'

'And the problem about a family?' David probed.

'She never mentions it. Neither do I. Why spoil something that's so wonderful? But I think about it a lot.'

'Problems sometimes solve themselves,' David said.

'Phone call for you, Chris,' the ward clerk shouted into the midwives' station. 'You can take it in my room if you want. I'm off for a coffee.'

It was later that day. The afternoon for once was slack and Chris was reading a tattered *Nursing Times*. Who could want him now? He ambled over to the ward clerk's little cubbyhole. 'Midwife Chris McAlpine here.'

'What time do you get home?'

The voice was cold, he didn't recognise it at first. Then… 'Joy! You're back, it's good to hear from you. I wasn't expecting you till tomorrow morning. I could have picked you up from the station.'

'I got a taxi, thank you. I asked you what time you were getting home.'

Now he recognised that something was wrong, seriously wrong. 'Joy. What's the matter? I can tell that you—'

'Just tell me when you get home!' Now she was really angry.

'Well, I finish here in about an hour and then it'll take me half an hour to get there. Are you coming to see me? That'll be great. But what's wrong? You sound—'

'I'll be waiting round the back of your house.' She rang off.

Perplexed and worried, he stared at the buzzing telephone. What was wrong with her? Her voice had been harsh, almost unnatural. Even when she'd been angry with him she'd never sounded like this. He shrugged. He would know soon enough.

Chris didn't go in through his front door, but walked round to the back where Joy had said she'd be waiting. He passed her car, and then she was there. Her back was to him. She was sitting on the patio where they'd spent so much happy time. His heart lurched when he saw that neat figure, the dark hair tied back. He hadn't seen her for three weeks. How could he have managed without her?

She was wearing trousers, a sweater, good clothes to travel in. He guessed she had come straight to see him. What was so important?

'Joy, it's so good to see you!' He walked over to her, tried to put his arms round her to kiss her. But she wriggled and pushed him away, pushed hard as if she meant it. 'Don't kiss me! Just sit in that chair and listen.'

He was unnerved. This was a new, frightening Joy. What had happened to her? 'Do we have to just sit here? Can't whatever it is wait till I've fetched us a drink?'

'No, it can't. I said sit down. And you can stop being so wonderfully thoughtful. I've had it with you being thoughtful.'

Something was seriously, dangerously wrong. Chris sat, looked at her. She wouldn't meet his glance, her eyes flicked everywhere but at him. 'Can't you at least look at me? I like looking at you.'

'I'll look at you when I need to. And what you like isn't important at the moment.'

'As you wish. I'll sit here silently till you tell me what's wrong.'

Now he was waiting it seemed as if she didn't know where to start. He saw her look at the sky, her twisting fingers, the end of the garden. Anywhere but at him. But he wouldn't speak. Now it was up to her.

'The first time you slept with me,' Joy said eventually, 'you told me…showed me the scars… You'd been in an explosion. You had to have surgery, and one result was that you couldn't father children.'

He felt sick. Was she going to end their relationship because he couldn't give her a family? Still…it was her right. 'Yes,' he said, his voice now as harsh as hers, 'I can't father children.'

'Then how come I'm pregnant?'

Chris stared at her, more shocked than he had ever been in his life. 'What?' It was all he could think to say.

'I said how come I'm pregnant?'

He couldn't take it in. For a moment the world around him ceased to exist, there was only him and this woman and that unbelievable question. 'Are you sure…?'

'My periods are never erratic. *Never!* I missed one and I couldn't believe it so I took a pregnancy test. Just as a joke, you understand.'

'You took a pregnancy test?' He knew he must sound like an idiot. But, then, he felt like one.

'Yes, a pregnancy test. You can buy them at the chemist's. And it was absolutely, finally, definitely positive.'

'But I don't understand,' he said weakly. 'You can't be… I mean you haven't…'

'Don't you dare suggest I've been with other men! Don't you just dare!'

'I wasn't going to. It's just that… You're really pregnant?'

'You're a midwife, you know how reliable tests are these days,' Joy said. 'In fact, I took a second test, just to make sure. Of course, it's early days yet…a lot can happen before the next few months are up. But as far as tests go, I'm pregnant. And I'm not very happy about it. In fact, I'm screaming mad! Chris, I trusted you! You told me you couldn't be a father and I believed you. Otherwise there was no way I would have let you make love to me without…without using something.'

'Please,' he begged, 'give me just a minute. I've got to get my mind round this, I've got to… Joy, you've changed my entire life.'

'Not as much as you've changed mine!' But she was silent for a while.

How could it have happened? He had seen the X-rays, talked to the surgeon, gone over his case time and time again with David Garner. Shrapnel splinters had cut through the vasa deferentia, there had been scar tissue there, there was no way he could father a child. But…he knew that in one case in uncounted many, a man who was in a similar situation had managed to become a father. Mother Nature corrected what was an insult to the human body. The surgeon had put the odds in his case at a million to one. And that million-to-one chance had come off.

'I must have been a complete fool,' Joy said. 'Tell me, Chris, how many women have you conned this way? How many women have you showed your scars to, told them this fairy-story? Did you do this on purpose?'

'No!' he said hoarsely, 'Joy, everything I told you was true—well I believed it was true. I believed it absolutely. Sweetheart, this is the best news I've ever heard! You're going to have a baby—our baby, yours and mine.'

'Yes, *I'm* going to have it. And I don't want it.'

'We'll get married,' he said, desperately trying to reassure her that he would be there for her. 'Every child should have a father. We'll get married.'

'No, we will not! I don't want to marry you, I don't think I even like you any more. I trusted you and you let me down!'

There was so much he had to think about, so much he knew he ought to say. He felt almost dizzy with conflicting emotions—but by far the greatest was delirious happiness. He was going to be a father. After so many years when he'd believed it was impossible. But…

Chris swallowed, tried to appear calm. 'Joy, this is as much a shock for me as it is for you. I think we've got to talk about things. Be reasonable, decide what's best for you…and the baby. But I can't hide the fact that I'm absolutely delighted. It's what I've dreamed of, but thought was impossible. And, really, the baby doesn't make any difference to how I feel about you. You must know I want to marry you, baby or no baby. So now we have to make decisions.'

'No!' The word was rapped out, terse and brutal. '*We* don't have to make decisions—*I* do. It's early days yet. I'll let you know what I've decided, if I think it's necessary.'

'But I want to—'

'I told you, what you want doesn't count for very much. I need to…I need to think. I didn't want this and…'

Finally her iron control collapsed, the tears ran down her face and her voice quavered, died away.

'Joy, sweetheart!' Chris stood, walked to put his arm round her.

'Don't you come near me! Don't you dare!' Now her voice was almost hysterical. His arm dropped and cautiously he walked back to his seat.

'I have to help,' he said. 'Whether you like it or not, this is my responsibility, too, and I'm going to face up to it.'

The silence between them seemed to stretch on to infinity. Finally she said, 'That's just what I thought you'd say. Well, I shan't be coming here again. We'll meet professionally, of course, but that will be all. I'll ask one thing of you, that you keep this secret. No one need know for the next couple of months—that'll give me time to think to work out what to do, how to organise my life. I suppose it's too much to ask you to leave hospital at once. To get out of my life for ever?'

'Yes,' he said. 'That is too much.'

'Then I'll call you for a talk in a couple of months.

Till then, no contact whatsoever. You understand what I'm saying?'

'I understand,' Chris muttered. He knew it was futile, but he felt he had to try again, to get her to see what he was feeling. But he knew it was a dangerous thing to do.

'Joy, I didn't plan this, I thought it could never happen. But it has and we have to deal with it together. You could make me so happy if we were married.'

'I'm not concerned with making you happy. I'm more concerned with keeping myself from being miserable.' Joy stood. 'I'll go now. Remember, say nothing to anyone. Is that understood?'

'Understood,' he said.

He could hide his troubles in work. The next day he was to be in Theatre with David again—three more Caesarean sections, all planned.

As usual, Chris was in Theatre first, he was to be scrub nurse. Dressed in his scrubs, he put ready the theatre packs, a set of instruments, two bowls, towels and drapes for each operation. Then he washed his hands for a good five minutes, lifting them so the dirty water always ran away from his fingers. His green gown was waiting and he thrust his hands into the sleeves, taking care only to touch the inside. He put on his latex gloves. Now Dora, a health care assistant and the theatre runner for the morning, came in and tied the back of his gown.

Time to go into the theatre. He opened the first theatre pack, put everything ready for David and then went into the anteroom to see the patient.

Sally Armstrong was already gowned and on the table. As the anaesthetist busied himself preparing for the first injection, Chris went over and smiled at the obviously nervous woman.

'Hi, I'm Chris McAlpine, I'm the midwife here. I'm going to be first to hold your baby, but you'll see her soon enough.'

'It's going to be a little boy,' the dry-lipped Sally said. 'I wanted to know so I asked after the scan. We're going to call him Sam. If it had been a girl we'd have called her Sally after me.'

Chris knew that many patients found it helped if they could talk when they were nervous. He always tried to keep up a flow of light conversation, keeping the woman from worrying about what was obviously an ordeal. He might officiate at a dozen sections a week, a woman had perhaps one or two in her life.

'I think Sam Armstrong sounds great,' he said. 'What's the name of the father?'

Sally managed a weak giggle. 'Percy,' she said, 'though he's known as Pip. We couldn't saddle a baby with that.'

'I like Pip Armstrong too. And if you have a little girl next, what about Phillipa?'

The anaesthetist came over, rubbed the back of Sally's hand with alcohol, and dextrously slipped in a cannula. All drugs would be administered through this. Chris smiled at the woman. 'When you wake up you'll have a baby,' he said.

Once Sally was in the theatre, David came in, said hello to everyone and bent straight to his patient. The other midwife who was to take the baby came in, too, checked the oxygen and suction on the Resuscitaire and accepted a sterile green towel from Chris.

Baby Sam was soon delivered. Chris leaned over and inserted a tube into the baby's mouth, gently sucking out any fluid. David handed the crying little figure to the midwife who carried it over to the Resuscitaire. All was well.

After that there were two more. It was satisfying work. The precision needed for the surgery didn't affect the obvious pleasure that all felt in the theatre. Chris lost himself in what he was doing, and for a while his own problems were forgotten. There were the tired but hopeful faces of the mothers, the creased little red faces of the babies. It made his life worthwhile.

'Another good job,' David said. 'We make a good team. By the way, I see Joy is back. Want to bring her round for dinner soon? Mary was asking about you both again.'

Chris had promised not to gossip. But talking to David wasn't gossip. Besides, he needed help. David was the best man he knew to confide in, the one man he knew who might help. 'Joy is pregnant,' he said flatly. 'Pregnant by me.'

'You! But, Chris, I saw the X-rays, saw the surgeon's report. It's just not possible.'

'Not possible or very, very highly unlikely?'

'Well the vasa deferentia were severed completely. But sperm production was fine, and I suppose that there's just the tiniest of chances... Chris, congratulations! You're a very lucky man.'

'Tell that to Joy. She's not very keen. She feels trapped, says that she doesn't like me very much and certainly won't marry me.'

'Ah. Want me to have a word with her?'

'I doubt it would do any good,' Chris said wearily. 'Besides, she made me promise to keep it secret.'

David thought for a minute. 'I guess you're in trouble,' he said.

*　　*　　*

Chris thought he would give Joy a week to cool down, and then try to re-establish some kind of relationship. He passed her a couple of times in the corridor, got a cold smile and no more. When he had to go to see her about the work he was doing, he found the shift leader already in her room. He could never see her alone.

After a week he phoned her in her office. 'We have to talk,' he said.

'There's nothing to talk about. I've got my life organised. And that organisation doesn't include you.'

'There are other people's lives here, too! If not mine, then the baby's!'

'The baby will do very well. She or he will have a loving mother, a doting grandmother.'

'But I need—'

She cut in. This was a new Joy, a harder one than he had ever met before. 'Any minute now you're going to tell me you've got rights. You're wrong, you're entitled to nothing, you have no rights. And if you try to push me you'll find you don't have a friend left in the hospital. I'm certain of that. And we'll see what the courts say about your so-called rights.'

'I'm sorry. Please, ring me when we can talk.' Chris rang off. He knew that newly pregnant women were often a little erratic in their moods—it was a common result of their hormonal imbalance. But Joy didn't seem erratic, she seemed coldly efficient.

He was left with one gloomy thought. Joy seemed to have developed a military mind of her own. That didn't please him at all.

CHAPTER EIGHT

ANOTHER two weeks passed and still Joy didn't phone him. Chris saw her in the distance but she seemed to be able to keep well way from him. He carried on with his work, listening carefully to the gossip of the other midwives—some of them appeared able to spot a pregnancy within hours of conception. But no one suspected what had happened to Joy. For her sake he was glad. In time she would have to see a doctor, think about antenatal classes and so on. Then the secret would be out. And he didn't want to listen to all the inevitable speculation about who the father might be.

Autumn was now well on its way. The nights were drawing in and it was getting cooler in the evenings. He thought he had never seen the moors more beautiful than in their russet colours. But for once he could draw no pleasure from them. He had problems that wouldn't go away.

It was a Wednesday evening, he had stayed late to cover part of another midwife's shift and now was driving home. He wasn't looking forward to it. At work he could lose himself, or even draw comfort from the fact that he was near Joy. At home he merely moped.

Nearly home. And there, parked outside the front of his cottage, was a Land Rover, if anything even more battered than his own. A great smile lit up Chris's face. Perhaps things weren't too bad.

Quietly, he pulled in behind the vehicle and gave a gentle toot on his horn. A man leaped out of the vehicle.

He was seemingly in his late fifties with greying hair, but still with the lithe movements of a much younger man. Chris stepped out, and the two men hugged each other. 'Hi, Dad,' Chris said. 'You don't know how good it is to see you.'

'I'm ready for a holiday,' the man replied, 'and it's good to see you, too.'

For the past few years Chris had only seen his father occasionally, but he was closer to him than to any other man. After the death of Chris's mother, James McAlpine had taken a desk-bound job that he'd hated and had looked after his only child with the devotion that perhaps only a single parent could give. And when Chris had turned eighteen, he'd said, 'You're a man now son.' Then he had gone to work abroad as a mining engineer. They wrote to each other once a week.

James was shown round the cottage, given the spare bedroom to sleep in and invited to have a bath to wash off the grime of the journey. 'Then we'll walk down to the pub for a meal and a pint,' Chris said. 'I feel in the mood for a small celebration.'

Their meal was a good one, and afterwards they sat companionably together, pints in hand, and looked at the view of the darkening sea.

'If it's all right, I need a home for a couple of weeks,' James said. 'But I can always find a hotel if it's not convenient.'

'Don't be silly! You stay with me.' Chris thought for a minute. 'You're not working, are you?'

Two years ago James had been injured in a roof fall. He had recovered, but slowly. Since then he hadn't spent as much time in the more dangerous jobs he had taken in his prime.

'It's sort of work,' James said, 'and it's near here.

You know they used to mine lead up on the moors—
they carried on until the late nineteenth century. Well,
they're thinking of reopening one and having it as a
museum. Trips round, mine your own bit of lead ore,
that kind of thing. And they want me to do an initial
safety check and report. You know, what needs replacing and so on. I'm quite looking forward to it.'

'Sounds fun. A man should always enjoy his work.'

James looked at his son closely. 'I know you enjoy
being a midwife, I think your house is wonderful, everything seems to be going fine for you. So why the
sudden gloomy voice?'

Chris should have known he couldn't hide much from
his father. 'How d'you fancy being a grandfather?' he
asked.

What James thought was obvious from the expression
on his face—he was delighted. 'You told me it was
impossible! But I can think of nothing better for you,
Chris, and I'm overjoyed. But do I gather there are
problems?'

'You could say that. It looks like we'll be father and
grandfather at a distance. Let me get us a couple more
drinks before I tell you.'

His father was a good listener and Chris had always
valued his advice. He told James everything—from the
first mysterious attraction between Joy and himself, the
way they'd got to know each other, their growing love
and then the apparently miraculous appearance of the
baby. And now her absolute refusal to talk to him.

Surprisingly, James could understand Joy's point of
view. 'She trusted you, son, and now she feels let down.
She sounds a proud girl, this is going to hurt her.'

'Thanks, Dad. All I needed was a bit of support.'

James slapped his son's shoulder. 'Something will

get sorted out, it always does. Where's this girl live? What family does she have?'

Chris told his father the little he knew. 'Apparently she lives with her widowed mother—I think she's called Anna, she's some kind of infant teacher. They live in a big semi but I've never been invited in. Number 28 Rathbone Road. I've considered calling round to see Joy but…perhaps it's wise not to.'

'How's her mother going to react to being a grand-mother?'

'I've no idea,' said Chris. 'The reaction of Joy's mother is the least of my worries.'

'She'll be delighted,' said James expansively, 'like I am. Now, I think we've drunk enough. What about this walk along the cliffs?'

Next day was work as usual but Chris enjoyed it more than he'd expected. His father would be waiting for him at home. In his time Chris had had to spend many sol-itary hours but now he actively didn't like his own com-pany. He wanted to share his life.

The Land Rover was outside the cottage. James had said that he would drive round the area, get to know it just as Chris had done. Evidently he'd finished his scouting tour.

Chris opened his front door and was about to shout a greeting when he heard a peal of laughter. A feminine peal of laughter. 'Dad?' he called, confused.

'Come in, son, we're having a cup of tea. There's one in the pot. I've got someone you have to meet.'

Chris entered his living room. There was a lady there, perhaps in her fifites. She was slim with a still youthful figure and dark hair, and wore a dark grey dress. He knew who it was the moment he saw the smile, the sparkle in her eyes.

'You're Joy's mother,' he said. There was nothing else he could say. He was dumbfounded. What was she doing here?

She stood and held out her hand. 'I'm Anna Taylor, and I'm pleased to meet you, Chris. I've heard nothing at all about you from my daughter, but your father has filled me in on a few details.'

'Has he?' Chris said. He shook the offered hand and then saw that his father was coming back with a cup from the kitchen. 'So I've got you to blame for this, Dad?'

James shrugged. 'You said you were getting nowhere so I decided to interfere. I'm acting purely selfishly. If there's a grandchild I want to see…her.'

'You paused, you thought,' Anna accused him. 'You changed what you were going to say.'

'I've never been sexist,' James said urbanely. 'I love all women.'

Chris sat down, accepting a cup from his father. 'This all seems a bit unreal,' he said. 'I'd be glad if someone would tell me what's going on.'

He saw James and Anna look at each other and smile. Then James said, 'You told me about you and Joy. It struck me that Joy's mother probably knew as well, and that meant we had something in common. So I phoned her and asked if we could meet for a talk. We had lunch in a café, found we had a lot to talk about. Anna had never met you so I invited her back here for tea.'

'I'll accept any interview or inspection,' Chris said gloomily. Then it struck him. When had Anna discovered that Joy was pregnant? Had she found out through his interfering father?

'You know I've been close to Joy,' he said, 'and that we've had some problems?'

'Two women in one house,' Anna said, 'I've known she was pregnant for a while, if that's what you mean. Anyway, she told me at once. But she's steadfastly refused to say anything about the father. I may be her mother, but she's always been a determined child.'

'I know that—how I know it.' He was discovering that he really liked this woman, she had a forthright approach that appealed to him. 'Are you going to help me, Anna?'

She looked at him assessingly for a while before answering. 'First thing, I won't go behind Joy's back. I'll tell her I've been here, tell her what I think of you. I'll also tell her that if I want to see you or your father again I shall do so.'

'I see Joy's not the only determined one,' Chris said.

'Quite. There are just two things I want to hear from you. I've heard them from your father, now I want you to tell me. First, was this a genuine accident? Second, do you really want to marry Joy?'

Chris sighed. 'I thought—I knew I couldn't have children. You've no idea what a thrill, what excitement it gave me when I found out that somehow I was going to be a father. But I suspect this will be the only chance.'

'I rather doubt that,' Anna said. 'In my experience lightning does strike twice in the same place.'

'It doesn't look like it'll strike twice with Joy. To answer your second question, yes, I do want to marry her. The trouble is, I don't think she likes me very much.'

'She's certainly not very happy at the moment,' Anna agreed. 'What d'you want me to do?'

'Just get her to talk to me. We have to talk, there's some things that must be settled. If nothing else, this is a responsibility and I'm going to play my part whether she likes it or not.'

'Not quite the right attitude to have at the moment,' said Anna, 'though I'm glad you said it. I'll have a word with her, exert my small maternal influence. Now, I think I'd better go.'

'I'll run you back,' said James with a smile.

Anna stood and kissed Chris quickly on the cheek. 'I must say, of the few men my daughter has brought for my inspection, I much prefer you.'

'Thanks,' said Chris. 'And I think you'd be a great mother-in-law.'

'We'll have a word when I get back, Chris,' his father said.

'I think we should.'

'I gather your father has been in touch with my mother,' the frigid voice said.

It was coffee-break time the next morning, and Chris was in the midwives' station. He tried to push himself even further into the telephone booth, yet not show what he was doing. He didn't want the other midwives to hear what he was saying.

'Yes,' he said. 'I'm sorry if it caused you any annoyance, it wasn't my idea.'

'I know that.' There was a pause. 'My mother was impressed with James, she's threatened to bring him round for tea to meet me. And she even quite liked you.'

'In spite of me being the kind of untrustworthy man I am,' Chris said, adding, 'Sorry, didn't mean that.'

'Yes, you did. But, anyway, my mother thinks it only

fair I at least talk to you. So I will. I'm not sure what
for, but I will.'

'Shall I come round to your house tonight?' Chris
asked hopefully.

'No. We'll meet on neutral ground. How about that
pub near you—the Fisherman's Arms?'

'All right. Shall I pick you up?'

'I do have my own car. Be there at half past seven.
I'll meet you in the car park. I'm not going to walk in
on my own.'

'Of course not,' he said.

As seemed to happen so often when Chris saw Joy, the
evening was a perfect one. The sun was low, the
slightest of breezes carried the scent of the moors. Chris
was there early—of course.

When Joy drove up she left her engine idling and
didn't get out of the car. He walked over to speak to
her and she said, 'It's too nice an evening to spend in
a smelly pub. I'd rather walk along the cliffs with you.
The same place as before?'

'Suits me fine,' he said. 'Shall we go in my car?'

'No. I know the way, you follow. We can both park
down there.'

There were no other cars at the end of the little road.
He got out, saw that she had walked over to the little
bluff to the wooden seat where she could look out to
sea. A moment later he joined her. Often Chris came
here himself. The beauty of the scene never failed to
calm him. Perhaps it affected her the same way. He
hoped so. But he felt a certain kinship as they stood
there in silence together. He made no attempt to
touch her.

'Let's walk a while,' he said. 'I can tell you don't want to talk yet.'

'Good idea. I need some fresh air, I've been in stuffy meetings all day.'

They set off together. Sometimes they could walk side by side on the grass of the clifftop, sometimes the path narrowed and he had to walk behind her. He could see the sheen of her hair, the confident swinging of her arms, the outline of the figure he knew so well, hidden by her shapeless anorak.

She was carrying his child. The sheer magic of it, the excitement was almost more than he could bear. Why couldn't she recognise what he felt, feel the same emotions he did? But perhaps in some way she did. He would have to be careful.

They walked for half an hour and then stopped where there was another bench with a view across the bay. The sea was silver. Only a few ships in the distance marred its stillness. They sat together and, greatly daring, he took Joy's hand. She didn't resist, but neither did she react.

'You wanted to talk,' she said.

Obviously she wasn't going to offer him any help, make any concessions. Chris didn't reply at once. He had spent all afternoon working out what he was going to say, and now he had the chance he still didn't know.

'Two things to get straight first,' he said. 'You do believe me when I say that you getting pregnant was an accident?'

'Yes. I guess so.'

'Second, do you know how much it means to me?'

Her answer this time was slower. 'I...suppose so. Usually you don't think of men as being so keen on having children. But in some ways you aren't an ordinary man.'

'So you see I have a problem?'

This was going too far. 'Not as much a problem as I have,' she snapped. 'Until I met you I was happy in my career, good at it, ambitious. I did want to have children perhaps at some date, but I wanted to get married, decide when I wanted to have children, be the kind of responsible person we're always trying to teach our mums to be. Instead of that, look at me. I've been caught! Had an accident. Been put upon by some smart-talking man. What d'you think the rest of the midwives are going to say?'

'You've got a good team and they think a lot of you. You'll have all their sympathy.'

'I don't want their sympathy! I want their respect! We may do all we can for our mums-to-be in this state—but you've heard the jokes behind their backs?'

Yes, he had heard the jokes. 'Not from all the midwives,' he said. This meeting wasn't going well. He would have to try to turn it round.

'I can still feel the attraction between us,' he said, 'and I think you can, too. We have such a lot in common.' He tried a gentle smile. 'I know that you're my boss, and that people joke about marrying the boss, but I think we would be great together.'

'Why? I agree you're an attractive man. I was even falling in love with you. But I'm not sure you want to marry me for the right reasons. And I'm not worried about being your boss because we both know you're going to rise rapidly through the ranks. Look how much you're enjoying working out these schedules and so on.'

Chris had no answer to that. He had been working very hard on the schedules—still was, in fact—and was seeing quite a lot of the CEO. The two men got on well together.

After a while Joy said, 'You're still asking me to marry you?'

'Yes, I am.'

'So you could be a good father to your—our child?'

'It would make me so happy,' Chris said. 'I would…' Then too late he saw how he had said the wrong thing. 'That is, I want to—'

She cut him short. 'You'd be marrying me, not the baby,' she said. 'And if that was a proposal, you left something out. You're supposed to say you love me.'

'Joy, you know I do,' he cried. 'It's just that—'

'It's just that you think other things are more important,' she said. 'Chris, if you love me, will you do anything for me?'

'Well, yes. More or less,' he said. He knew how weak, how feeble his answer seemed, but he saw the trap she was leading him into.

'Well, I'll tell you what you can do if you love me. Leave. I'll bring up the baby. I don't need you. The two of us will be happy together.'

'You know I can't do that! I must have some knowledge of you and the baby. I need to know!'

'So your needs, your feelings come first?'

How could he explain to her how he felt? That she meant the world to him—and not just because she was carrying his child. 'I want what's best for you, for the baby and for myself last,' Chris muttered.

'I think we've finished talking. Shall we go back now?'

They walked back in silence. Joy got into her car, then opened the window to look at him.

'I'm not boasting,' he said, 'I don't want to. But people have said I've got a quick mind. I can work out chances, techniques, ways round problems. But now I've got the biggest problem of my life and I can't think of anything to do except to hope that you'll change your mind. Can we talk again some time?'

'I expect so,' she said, 'but don't get your hopes up. You said yourself you thought that the point of marriage was having children. Well, I want a man who wants me, not just my baby.'

She drove away quickly then, the side of her car pushing him away. He felt as if his emotions had been battered. He decided to go and have a drink with his father.

It was different, but Chris was enjoying himself. He was walking down a narrow tunnel, following James. A battery fastened to his belt led to a light on his hard hat, and the light glistened on the black walls of the rock on each side.

'The first miners came down here with just candles in their hatbands,' his father said. 'Things got better, of course, but mining was always a hard life. Now, there's a scramble down here but it's quite an easy gradient.'

'It's a good thing that I'm not claustrophobic,' Chris said.

They were walking down the mine that James was surveying. He had suggested that if Chris was feeling low, then a change of scenery might be a good idea. Not that there was much scenery. Just rock, scarred here and there by pick marks.

'Are you serious about this being a tourist attraction, Dad?'

'Why not?' His father seemed to think the question an odd one. 'Near Malton there's a German POW camp you can visit. People like to see how hard things were, makes them appreciate what's good in life. And this is a safe mine. Just a few precautions and some staircases built and the public'll flock here.'

Chris suppressed a smile. His father was an enthusiast about mines.

They entered a high chamber, with no obvious way out. His father pointed up the side of the chamber, to where there was the opening of another passage. 'Now, this is where we're going to need a wooden stair built. There's a ladder here now. It's all the miners used but I guess tourists can't possibly be asked to climb that.'

'You really expect people to pay to come down here?'

'I'm sure they will.' Chris watched his father run nimbly up the ladder, then turn at the top. 'Come on up. You can see the actual seam here. We're going to lend people picks and let them chip out their own ore.'

'The things people will do,' Chris said, carefully climbing the ladder. He was enjoying the trip, hearing of the plans for the mine—a café, a souvenir shop. But all he seemed to think about was Joy.

It was something new for Chris, part of Joy's policy of getting all her staff to take part in different aspects of the unit's work. Yes, this was something definitely new. For two days he was to be lent to a team that travelled round the local schools, lecturing on sexual health, birth control, and so on.

'This is the programme,' said Leonard Astley, the rather ineffectual leader of the team. 'There are the slides here, and this is what the talk is about.'

'Does the talk go down well?' Chris asked.

Leonard sighed. 'There's a lot of…rather racy humour. Children have changed since we were at school.'

'I doubt that,' said Chris. He leafed through the material he had been given. 'I'm going to add my own input to this.'

'But that's the programme!' Leonard gasped.

'And I suspect it didn't do much good,' said Chris.

After the two days he was called in to see Joy. For once they were on their own. She had no midwife or shift leader as chaperone.

'I've had a complaint about you—of sorts,' she said. 'I thought this was a straightforward job. I know you're a good speaker, I know you know your stuff. All you had to do was show the slides and then present the facts to the children. But Mr Astley said you departed… considerably from the programme.'

'There are two aims to that programme,' Chris said. 'One is to get through to kids—in the most sexually potent time of their lives—that sex should be part of a relationship, not an end in itself. The second is that if they're going to have sex anyway, to make sure they know enough about contraception to ensure there are no…unnecessary accidents.'

'A fine pair to talk about that, aren't we?' she asked with a wan smile. 'In fact I agree with you. But Mr Astley feels you departed too far from the script. And he wrote it.'

'That figures. What did the children think of the talk?'

'Ah. After I heard from Mr Astley, I phoned the headmistress of High Moors School. She thinks you're marvellous. You handle a mixed audience well, you got the kids thinking and talking. You're the best we've ever sent, and can you come back?'

'Great,' said Chris. 'I can tell a bunch of kids how to organise their love lives, but I can't even get my own right.'

'Better listen to one of your own lectures,' cooed Joy.

He was here with her alone, he had to seize his chance. 'So while we're on the subject, what about us?' he demanded.

'I don't know. I'm still thinking. My life's about to be turned upside down. I don't know that you would make it any more pleasant.'

His pager bleeped, he was needed. 'I have to go,' he said. 'Will we talk again?'

'Perhaps,' she said.

Chris set off to answer his call. Perhaps she was mellowing a little. But he still didn't know.

Fortunately he wasn't busy the next afternoon. The shift leader called over to him, slightly surprised. 'I've just had a message from David Garner. If you can be spared, will you meet him over at A and E? And quickly, please.'

Chris looked equally surprised. 'I'm on my way,' he said. 'Bleep me if I'm needed back here.'

He hurried over and saw the spare figure of David waiting for him outside the A and E entrance. 'I've just been called over here,' David said, 'a sort of courtesy call, I suppose. Chris, Joy Taylor's been in an accident.' He saw the panic on Chris's face and said quickly, 'It's all right, she's going to live and it could have been much much worse.'

'What happened?' Chris asked thickly.

'Some scaffolding collapsed in the high street and

caught her. Apparently Joy saw it moving, tried to hurry a group of kids along.'

Chris went white with shock. Once he had been used to hearing of men, friends even, being injured or sometimes killed. You took it, didn't show any emotion. But this was different. He hadn't realised how much it could hurt.

'Tell me she's going to be all right!'

'Well, the A and E consultant thinks so. Fortunately the pipes missed her face, but there are lacerations to the scalp—no sign of concussion, though. She has a broken arm and is badly bruised.'

Chris studied his friend. 'There's more, isn't there?'

David sighed. 'I'm afraid so. The reason I was sent for. There's vaginal bleeding, Chris. You know what this means—possible spontaneous abortion.'

Chris swayed as if struck. 'She might lose the baby?'

'It's very possible. You're a midwife, you know that many babies never progress beyond three months. But we're not sure yet.'

'You've got to do something!'

'Chris, we're doing everything we can! But at the moment all we can do is wait and hope. You know this as well as I do.'

Somehow Chris gained control of himself. 'Of course,' he said quietly. 'Bed rest is the only thing. Now, can I see her?'

He turned to walk inside but David held him back. 'I'm not sure that's a good idea. You told me that your relationship was a bit…uncertain. I don't want her more upset. But I'll ask her if she wants to see you. Incidentally, her mother's on her way.'

Chris's first reaction was to tell David to go to hell, he was going in anyway. But then the logic of what his friend had said slowly came clear. He had to think of Joy. Not himself.

David looked even more upset. 'There's another thing, Chris. You know hospitals. It's going to come out that Joy is pregnant. There will be rumours, questions. She'll have to deal with that, and it's got to be her choice as to how she does it. Not your choice! Now, get back to the unit, tell them what has happened and say that I'll be in touch with any news the minute there is any.'

Joy's—and the baby's—welfare. Her choice as to what she did. Her decision as to whether she wanted to see him. His needs, his feelings had to come last. But it was hard! He knew that what David had said was absolutely true. He desperately wanted to see her. But he wasn't certain that she wanted to see him.

'I'll get back,' he said. 'Thanks for calling me over, David.'

Chris walked back to the unit, told the shift leader what had happened. The shift leader was appalled and very concerned—and promptly reached for the telephone to call a very close friend in A and E. Chris sighed. There was no keeping secrets in a hospital.

Perhaps it was a good thing that he was called then to go and assist at a birth. He thought it wouldn't be possible for him to concentrate but, of course, he could. He was a midwife. He had a job to do.

When he had finished in the delivery room he walked back to the station—and there was David, talking to the shift leader. He had to steel himself to walk up casually, to pretend only a friendly interest.

'Everything with Joy is fine, Chris,' David said, 'I mean *everything*—so far.'

Chris understood the coded message. The baby was fine—so far.

David finished talking to the shift leader and then said, elaborately casually, 'If you've got a couple of minutes, Chris, I'd like to see you in my office.'

'Think I can manage that,' Chris said.

The two faced each other in David's office. 'First of all,' David said, 'Joy Taylor is now my patient. You know as well as I do that I can't talk about her without her permission. But…as I said before, she's badly bruised, has head lacerations and a compound fracture of the humerus. With a break like that she'll need to be admitted. Then she's going to need some weeks off, but these things are eminently curable. I have given her a careful examination and then an ultrasound scan. The foetal heart rate is fine. That means there's an excellent chance that the baby is fine and everything will be all right. The baby doesn't appear to be harmed.'

Chris bowed his head, unable to speak. It was better news than he could have expected. The relief was almost unendurable. 'That's good,' he said. 'May I go to see her?'

David looked grave, stared straight at Chris. 'I know Joy quite well,' he said. 'I would call her my friend. We had quite a long conversation, in private. Although she was distressed and in pain, in my opinion she was quite aware of what she was saying. She asked me to bring a message to you. She still doesn't want to see you. When she does, she'll be in touch. And she recognises that everyone will know about the baby now, she knows there will be gossip. She says she's entitled to ask that you say nothing, and if you're asked—you deny all knowledge of the baby.'

Chris fought to keep calm, a rage so hot burning inside him that he could hardly speak. When he finally did force out the words, his voice was unrecognisable.

'I will do no such thing. That child is mine and I will…' Then he stopped. What would he do?

He heard the chink of glass on glass. From a locked drawer in his desk David had taken a bottle and two glasses. He poured a small measure into each one. He pushed a glass across to Chris. 'I *never* drink on duty,' he said, 'but here's what I would drink if I did.'

Chris sipped. A single malt whisky, peaty and smoky, with a taste that lingered long after it was swallowed. The two men drank in silence. Chris felt that his thudding heart was slowing and he could think reasonably again.

'She's said she doesn't want to talk to me before,' he said. 'But I thought she was coming round a bit.'

David nodded, his face still bleak. 'Sudden trauma like this accident can alter people's perception of what's right, what's best for them. When she's fully recovered…who knows? She may think again. But, Chris, she knew what she was saying, she was quite rational. In the interests of her future health—and the well-being of the baby—I think you have to do as she wishes.'

Chris rocked in his chair. How much more did he have to take? 'Of course,' he said. 'But you will…?'

'I'll keep you informed,' David said. 'Just don't tell people I'm doing it.'

CHAPTER NINE

'FANCY our Joy having a baby,' the first midwife said comfortably the next day. 'Who'd have thought it? Any-one any idea who the father is?'

'Someone said something about a man she met on this course in London,' the second midwife said. 'Chris, have you any idea who the father might be?' This was said in a half-challenging way.

It was the next afternoon, in the station. As Chris had known it would, the story had spread with incredible speed and everyone was gossiping.

He shrugged, decided to accept the challenge. 'Well, it certainly wasn't me,' he said. 'I don't think she likes male midwives very much.' He had thought about this all night. Joy had asked him not to talk about their re-lationship. He would accept her wishes.

'She's been against them since the last one,' the first midwife agreed. 'But you're a lot better. Here, sign this and give me a couple of pounds. We're going to send her some flowers and chocolates.'

Chris took the large card. Everyone in the unit had signed it, written a message. Joy was popular. He wrote, 'Missing you, come back soon, love Chris.' No one could find anything unusual in that. He hoped that Joy would understand what he was feeling.

'Nice,' said the second midwife, reading what he had written. 'Perhaps she'll be more in favour of male mid-wives now.'

'I doubt it,' said Chris.

The shift leader came over, a note in her hand. 'Chris, could you go over and see the CEO at half past four? In the committee room, he wants to talk to you. I'll see you're covered.'

'Ooh!' said the first midwife. 'Who's got influential friends, then?'

'It'll be those schedules I sent over to him,' Chris said wearily. 'Quite frankly I could do without any more aggravation now. Still…I volunteered.'

The CEO was waiting for him in the committee room. There also, to Chris's surprise, was David Garner and a harassed-looking woman he recognised as Mavis Shaw, the human resources manager.

The CEO was businesslike. 'Mr McAlpine, I feel you've made an excellent impression during your time here. You know I particularly like your ideas about re-scheduling, and we'll be talking further about them. I gather you were elected unanimously as the midwives' representative?'

'Only because none of them wanted the job.'

'Quite. Mr Garner here tells me you have experience of leadership—though in a different field. You find management problems interesting?'

'Yes,' Chris said uneasily, 'but I came here to be a midwife.'

'You know Miss Taylor was injured yesterday. And now we find she's pregnant. I don't see her being able to bring her full attention to her job for quite a few months. However, she assures me that she will return eventually—for which I am very glad.'

The CEO glanced at David and Mavis. Both stared back at him and Chris saw David nod slightly. The CEO said, 'Will you take over Miss Taylor's responsibilities until she can return? Be acting head of the unit?'

Chris looked at him in shock. 'I can't do that! There are many more experienced people in the department who would be better at the job. Perhaps in a few years, but...'

The CEO smiled a weary smile. 'You don't know the conditions. First, there will be no extra money. Second, you will have to do quite a lot of your own work as well as the extra. I believe you'll be first rate at the job, but I wouldn't have dreamed of asking you. However, Mr Garner said you would take the job.'

Chris looked at the three faces opposite him. 'What does Miss Taylor think?' he asked.

'It's not really for her to decide,' the CEO replied, 'but I suspect she would be pleased to know her unit was in good hands.'

Chris was going to say yes. But he knew better than to take a decision like this too quickly. 'May I give you my answer tomorrow?' he asked. 'There may be a few conditions of my own.'

'Come and see me any time,' said the CEO.

When Chris got home that night he found his father about to go out to pick up Anna from the hospital. Quickly he told him about the offer he'd had.

'You've always been good with people, son,' James said. 'If the hospital needs you, then you've got to do the job.'

If the hospital needs you. He hadn't thought of it that way. But his father was right. 'We'll talk about it later.'

He looked at his father critically. James was wearing a white shirt, dark suit, and in his lapel a flower from Chris's garden matched a bright floral tie. He looked ten years younger than he was. With a smile, Chris asked, 'Dad, you're getting to see quite a lot of Anna. Are you looking after my interests or your own?'

'I'd like to think they were the same. At the moment Anna has a lot to worry about with Joy. I hope I can help her.'

'Everyone knows Joy is pregnant, Dad, but she doesn't want me to be known as the father.'

'You told me once that in some situations the best thing to do is nothing. And it's the hardest thing. This is one of those times.'

'I'd like to be acting head of department,' Chris told the CEO next day. 'I'm prepared to work extra hours. I've got nothing much to occupy my time. I'll start by organising a set of meetings with the staff and telling them what I propose. If there's any really strong opposition then I'll resign at once. But once I'm in the job I'll stick to it.'

'I think you'll be good. Joy Taylor will be really pleased with you.'

'I'm sure she will,' said Chris.

He had done this before. He couldn't do anything for Joy so he would lose himself in work. The first thing he did was organise another meeting of as many of the midwives as he could get together. This meeting would be all-important. If he could get the goodwill of the midwives, he would be all right for a few weeks.

'I'd rather Joy was doing this job,' he started, 'but I've accepted it and I want to do it right. There are three things I want to say. First, I don't get any extra money out of this. Second, I hope and intend to do as much of my normal midwifery duties as I can. Third, if anyone wants to come and see me about anything, I hope they will. Anything said will be in complete confidence. If there are complaints—and I'm sure there will be—then I want them made to my face. Now, about these new shift patterns…'

'It seems strange, telling my boss what to do,' Alice McKee said two days later. 'I feel I should be asking you, not telling you.'

Chris shook his head. 'We both know you've got far more clinical experience than me,' he said, 'and, don't forget, I'm still hoping to learn.'

'There's not much left that I can teach you,' said Alice, 'but it's good to have someone recognise what you're trying to do.' She handed Chris a pile of duty notes she had just filled in. 'Did you mean it when you said we could talk to you in complete confidence?'

'Yes, I meant it.'

'Even if it could seem a bit, well, unprofessional?'

Chris pondered. 'If the ultimate aim is the good of the patient then I want to know.'

'Di Owen. She's not a bad midwife when she's here,' said Alice, 'but she's not here enough. The number of times she's phoned in sick—and at the last minute. You know her husband's a doctor here, so she thinks she can get away with anything. And all the time off! Ill indeed! She's visiting that young sister of hers in Leeds.'

'What? Can you prove that?'

'I can't prove it,' Alice said gloomily, 'but I know it's true. For a while Di was matey with a pal of mine who's left now. Di told my pal, my pal told me. Of course, you couldn't accuse her without proof.' Alice thought over what she'd just said. 'You won't say anything, will you, Chris? Don't involve me, I've got to work with her.'

'Oh, I won't involve you,' said Chris.

Alice relaxed. 'Heard from Joy?' she asked happily. 'I thought it time I phoned her again.'

'I'm pleased to hear that,' Chris said, managing to control his natural feelings. 'She was a good boss to me.'

'We still don't know who the father of the baby is,' Alice pressed on, 'and we'd all love to know. Just so long as it's not that Henry Trust.'

Chris repressed a shudder. 'I think she'd have more sense than that,' he said.

For a moment an urge rushed over him to tell everyone just who the father was. But he resisted. He had given Joy his word, he would stick to it.

Alice sighed. 'Anyway, Joy thought she'd be away from work for quite a while. She's going to add some holiday time on top of her sick leave.'

Not see Joy for ages? Chris shivered, but he merely said, 'Sounds a good idea.'

The aim was to lose himself in work. He thought of Alice's bit of information, thought of the few times he had met Di Owen himself, remembered the half-hidden comments of the other midwives. Maybe he could get to the bottom of this.

Chris went to Joy's—his—office and unlocked the filing cabinet. He took out the file on Di Owen, read it through and winced. She'd had more than six times as much time off work through illness as any other midwife.

That night he asked his father if he would ask Anna to phone him. 'I need to have a word about work, Dad, but I don't want to upset Joy.'

Next morning, as he was sitting in Joy's office, Anna did phone him. Chris could tell that she was still shocked—frightened even—at what had happened

'Chris, if that scaffolding had hit her full on the head, she would have been dead. What would I have done then? I can't bear to think about it.'

'It didn't kill her,' Chris snapped. 'Anna, be positive. Your daughter had a horrible experience but she's alive and recovering. Don't concentrate on what might have been, but on what is!'

'Yes, Chris,' said Anna after a while. 'It's good to hear that and I suppose you're right. Tell me, how did you feel when you heard she'd been injured?'

'Just like you,' he admitted. 'Life seemed too full of horror. I wanted to hang onto what I had.'

'Quite,' said Anna. 'Chris, James said you wanted to talk to me.'

'I need to talk to Joy. Not about...not about us but about the job. You know I'm standing in for her?'

'We know. When Joy heard she said she thought you'd be good at the job. You'd be drilling the mid-wives every morning.'

'That comes next,' Chris agreed. 'Look, don't push her, but there are a couple of things here I need to discuss. Tell her...it's just the job.'

'Just the job,' Anna agreed. 'I'm sure she'll phone you, Chris, but it'll be about a week. She's still very...shaken up.'

'I know,' said Chris. 'I've seen what trauma can do to people.'

It was well into the evening just over a week later when the phone rang. He was in his office, there were some figures he had to check. Carelessly he reached for the handset. 'McAlpine here.'

'Hello, Chris, it's Joy here,' he heard, and his senses reeled. He just hadn't been expecting it, he told himself, it was just that he was surprised. But for a moment he couldn't speak. 'Joy, how are you?' he managed to stammer after a few seconds.

'I'm much better, thank you. But I don't want to talk about me—or you. This is about the job, it's a business call.'

Her coolness shocked him, but he was determined not to show it. 'If that's what you want, then fine. But just tell me…if I can't ask you about yourself, is the baby all right?'

There was a pause. 'Yes, the baby's doing fine. David's been round a couple of times, I've seen my GP and the community midwife and I've started antenatal care. It's fun.'

'It's different when you're actually involved, isn't it?' he asked gently. 'All those things you must have taught a dozen times—now they're real.'

Then her voice was cold again. She didn't want him to pry, didn't want him to be involved. 'What happened with Di Owen? Mavis Shaw phoned me and told me that you'd sorted it out. It's the best news I've had in months.'

'I talked to Di, and we both agreed it would be best for her if she resigned. She can do some occasional work on the bank, rather than committing herself to full-time work.'

'That's not good enough! Tell me exactly what you said!'

He hesitated for a moment then decided. After all, it was Joy's unit, not his. 'Di phoned in sick again a week ago, said her husband was treating her. She was confined to her bed, we weren't to phone her. She came back after four days and I called her in to interview said I wasn't happy with her performance, would she confirm in writing that she had been sick at home in bed. She wrote me a note at once. When I had the note, seen she'd signed it, I told her that I'd heard that she'd been to her sister's place in Leeds.'

'I see,' said Joy.

'At first she tried to deny it, and then she burst into tears. I told her I didn't want to sack her, that every problem had a solution and why didn't she talk to me. So she did. It turns out that her sister is an invalid. She's part paralysed and has got emotional problems as well—she phones up threatening suicide and demanding that Di come to see her. And so Di feels she has to go at once.'

'I didn't know that,' Joy said, 'I wish I had done.'

'It took some getting it out of her. But now it's done and Di feels much better. I've promised her a lot of bank work, she can turn that down if her sister's acting up. And I also said that we'd be in touch with Leeds and see if we couldn't get extra psychiatric help for her sister.'

'Quite the little social worker, aren't you?'

Chris lost his temper at this, just a little. 'Joy, because of what I did we have a tighter department and more comfortable mums, and that means more contented babies. And, just as importantly, Di Owen is happier and perhaps her sister will be, too.'

There was a pause that seemed endless, so eventually he said, 'I'm sorry to speak my mind.'

'No, I'm the one that should be sorry. You acted like the best kind of boss. You were quite right in what you did. Now, what else do we have to discuss about work?'

Chris couldn't work after that. It was late anyway so he went home. James had cooked supper and after they had eaten together he said that they had to talk.

'I've been offered a job at the mine, Chris. I'm very interested, I think I'll take it. I don't fancy wandering the world any more and I like it round here. In a couple of days I'll start looking round for a house or flat or something.'

'I'd rather you stayed with me,' Chris said mildly. 'I like having you around. But are the job and the area the only two reasons you want to stay?' He grinned at his father's slight discomfiture.

'No, Chris. I'm staying because of Anna. Both of us are a bit wary. But we think we've got something worth fighting for.'

'You're doing well for yourself, Dad. I really like Anna. And just think—you might become a grandfather without me becoming a husband.'

'Yes,' James said heavily. 'Well, there'll be nothing between Anna and me until her daughter's problems are sorted out. Incidentally, Anna likes you very much, but she has to look out for Joy.'

Two weeks later, autumn was sliding towards winter. When Chris left the hospital it was an evil night, the wind thrashing the rain against his windscreen. The bad weather suited his mood.

He felt tired and just a bit depressed. He wanted his relationship with Joy to go somewhere. He would so much like to be with her now. This should be a good time for her, he wanted to share in her happiness.

He had spent the day among excited mums-to-be, the occasional happy but apprehensive face of a dad-to-be. He had listened in on whispered plans, discussions about names. It was a good time for the families, and he wanted to be part of one himself. But he couldn't push Joy. He didn't know how she'd react.

There was a supper waiting for him and a note from James—he was out with Anna, might be back late. Chris grinned slightly sadly. He hadn't seen his father so happy in years. He wanted that kind of happiness himself. He ate his supper and went to bed early.

For a while he listened to the sound of the rain on the roof. He wasn't afraid of sleep now. Since that one last time with Joy the torment of his old nightmare had never returned. Being with her—or perhaps just explaining it to her—had cured him. He owed her so much for that—not that she'd be interested.

He'd had a hard day. He closed his eyes and slept.

The phone by his bedside rang and he was awake at once. He'd never lost the ability to wake and be instantly alert. He blinked at the bedside clock, saw it was half past two in the morning. 'McAlpine here.'

'Chris—it's Joy.'

Now he was tense. What could she be doing, phoning at this time? And her voice sounded strange, strained even. 'Joy. Are you all right? Is there anything wrong with the baby?'

She was impatient. 'Don't fuss. I'm fine and the baby is, too. If not I would have phoned the hospital. You know James went out with my mother?'

'Yes, he left me a note. But they're out nearly every night.'

'Well, they're not back yet.'

This was unusual. 'Hang on a minute.' He pulled on his dressing-gown, padded down to his father's bedroom and found it empty. He frowned and walked back. 'They're both old enough and sensible enough to know what they're doing,' he said when he returned. 'I shouldn't worry.'

'I'm not going to worry about my mother's sex life. I have enough trouble with my own. My mother hasn't phoned me, and if she was staying out late she would have done so. I've tried to phone her on her mobile and I've tried James's mobile number. There's no answer on either—for some reason both phones are dead. I've phoned the police and the hospitals and there's been no accidents reported. But they might have… Chris, I'm worried.'

'I'm coming round,' said Chris. 'I'll be there in fifteen minutes. Now, don't worry!'

'I knew you'd say that.'

He dressed quickly in boots, walking trousers, sweater and anorak. He hadn't seen Joy in a while, he calculated she must now be into her second trimester. As he drove—fast but not dangerously—his mind went through what was happening to her body. He had witnessed it so many times, he knew it all. But it felt so different when it was your baby involved.

She must have been looking out for him because the door opened before he could ring the doorbell. She was dressed to go out herself, in sweater and trousers. He couldn't help it. His eyes fell to her front where he knew there was a child—his child.

As happened to many women, pregnancy had made her even more beautiful. Her glossy hair shone with good health, her face was a little pale but more wonderful than ever.

Chris couldn't help himself. 'You look well,' he said. 'You look beautiful.' There was the mole on her face and for some reason that tiny imperfection made her seem even more desirable. Love held him so tight that he didn't know what else to say. 'I've missed you,' he managed at last. 'Have you missed me at all?'

'Well, I...' Then she stopped. 'Where's my mother and your father?' she asked.

'Get in the car. The fact that neither phone is working is a good thing.'

'But where are you taking me?'

'We're going looking up on the moors,' he said.

Three quarters of an hour later he turned off the main road onto a smaller one, and then off that onto a rough track. Outside it was still raining, and in the distance they could just hear the boom of the sea.

'Where is this place?' she asked. 'You haven't brought me up here to—?'

'This is the old mine where my father works. I can think of only one reason why both mobiles aren't working—because the owners are deep underground.'

'They might be hurt! We should phone the police, get—'

'Joy, don't worry. My father is a safety officer, he'd do nothing to endanger Anna. And I— Ah, I thought so.'

They drove into the mine car park. And there ahead of them was James's car.

The outer door to the mine was open. Chris flicked on the light and led Joy to where the lamps and hard hats were kept. He looked at her doubtfully. 'You could always wait in the car,' he said, 'I'm not sure if—'

'Chris, I'm coming. That's my mother in there. Don't treat me as if I'm made out of porcelain.'

'No, ma'am. Not claustrophobic, are you?'

'At the moment I'm getting more and more McAlpine-phobic. Just show me how to fit this light and then let's go.'

He remembered the route easily. In fact, there was nowhere to go wrong. They followed the main gallery.

He would have liked to have held her hand, but there wasn't really room for the two of them to walk side by side. So he led her, and watched the two little circles of light from their helmets dancing on the dark walls. After a couple of hundred yards they came to a bend and as they rounded the curve they saw another light ahead.

Chris walked into the high chamber he remembered, Joy close behind him. On the floor was a ladder and above them, at the beginning of the continuation gallery, there were two lights. 'Hi, Dad,' Chris called. 'Everything OK?'

'No real problem, son. What kept you?'

'Mum, are you all right? I was worried, I didn't know what had happened and I...' Joy's voice cracked. Chris realised just how upset she was.

'I'm all right Joy,' came Anna's calm voice. 'Just a small mishap. It was my fault, I kicked the ladder away. I'm sorry to put you to this trouble.'

'No trouble! It's just that—'

'Chris, the ladder fell after we got up here and we couldn't get back down,' James said. 'If you could prop it up against the wall, we'll come down and join you.'

Chris saw Joy bend to pick up one end of the ladder. Firmly he took it from her. 'You don't lift heavy weights,' he said. 'Now, stand by the wall while I get this up.'

'But I want to—'

'Just stand there. I'll get your mother down.' Quietly, Joy did as she was told.

Chris easily swung the ladder into place, and after he had done so James tied the top rung to a spike driven into the rock. Then Anna carefully climbed down, and James came after her.

Joy flew tearfully into her mother's arms. 'Ma! Do you know what you put me through? I thought you were dead, I thought you'd had an accident.'

Anna stroked her daughter's hair. 'There, sweetheart, don't worry. It didn't happen, I'm fine.'

'I wondered what I'd do without you.'

'Well, you won't have to. Now, come on, it's been quite interesting sitting up there talking to James, but I think we should all go home now.'

'I'll lead the way,' said James. 'Chris, you bring up the rear.'

The two women were still holding each other tightly as James passed Chris. 'Some safety officer you are,' muttered Chris. 'Letting a woman climb a ladder that hasn't been tied down.'

'Accidents will happen,' James said urbanely. 'And sometimes they have a happy ending.' He raised his voice. 'Come on, ladies. We'll soon be home to a hot drink and bed.'

He led the way out. Chris had one last glance at the wall, at the ladder—now tied down. Strange, he thought.

They drove back home in the cars they had come in, Anna with James, Joy with Chris. Chris kept quiet as they bumped slowly over the rough path, but spoke once they were on the main road. 'You've had a hard night—try to sleep,' he said.

'I'll sleep in tomorrow morning. But I'm still wide awake, my thoughts are churning. Chris, you weren't as worried as I was, were you?'

'I worked out what had most likely happened,' he said. 'But I could have been wrong.'

'I was worried. I was worried for Ma, of course—but I kept on wondering—what would I do if I was alone in the world? No mother, alone in the world with a baby to bring up.'

'If you married me you wouldn't be alone. I really wish you would.'

Somehow she laughed. 'Not exactly the most passionate of declarations I've heard. But what you say is true…I suppose.'

'I can be passionate,' he said, 'you know I can be passionate. And I know you can be, too. But now… Joy, I was wrong before about kids being the point of marriage. It's you I want…but I just can't help thinking of that tiny bulge inside you as well.'

Somehow he knew she was smiling. 'There's a layby ahead, pull in,' she said. Then she unzipped her anorak, reached down to her waist under her sweater.

When they had stopped she took his hand, guided it over her newly bared abdomen. 'There, feel that,' she said.

Of course, it was something he had done so often before with mums-to-be. But when Chris felt the warmth of her skin, smelled the faint freshness of her, it was so new, so different. And then, almost imperceptible, he felt a movement, a kick, in fact. 'That's…your child,' he said.

Joy recognised the effort he'd made to say what he thought she would want. 'Well he—or she—has a father, I suppose,' she said.

He kept his hand there, blissfully happy. Then he said, 'Joy, I—'

She leaned over, kissed him on the cheek. 'I'm tired,' she said. 'I've had enough emotion for one day. But I'll listen to what you have to say soon. I'll phone you, I promise.'

'That's fair enough,' he said. 'So long as it's quite soon.'

Two days later Chris was in his office. At long last, after many hours' work, he had worked out a new shift system and confirmed it with the CEO. Both were quietly pleased with it. People would have to make small sacrifices, perhaps lose privileges, but no one would have to be made redundant. And no one would lose money.

There was a knock on the door. He shouted, 'Come in.' But he didn't look up. 'One second,' he mumbled. 'Just this last calculation and—'

'Hello, Chris,' said Joy. He looked up, and the calculations were suddenly totally unimportant.

'Joy!' He stood, rushed round his desk, his arms outstretched. Then he hesitated and looked at her cautiously. His arms lowered. Their last meeting had been, well, reasonably friendly, she had kissed him on the cheek. But he knew she had been upset at the possibility of losing her mother. Things between them were far from how they had been before she'd fallen pregnant.

'I'll make some coffee,' she said, moving towards the little machine on the table in the corner. 'You take your nose out of those figures and read the article on page fifty-seven.' She threw a copy of the *British Medical Journal* on the desk.

'You can't just come in here and ask me to read a magazine,' muttered Chris, pushing it away. 'You can certainly make me a coffee if you want, but we've got other things to talk about than an article in the *BMJ*.'

'Page fifty-seven. Skim it if you like—it'll only take you a couple of seconds. It's something I came across quite by chance.'

So Chris took the magazine, opened it and skimmed the article. Then he sat back and read it through, slowly, carefully, twice. Even Joy was forgotten for the moment and the coffee grew cold by his elbow. 'Very interesting,' he said. For some reason he felt he had to keep his excitement down. After all, he had been disappointed before.

'I know about your case, you even showed me your case notes,' said Joy. 'So after I'd read that article I phoned the surgeon who had written it and asked him a couple of hypothetical questions. He thinks it very possible—especially since you've now fathered one child—that your condition could be reversed. It's over five years since you were injured, there have been some great advances in microsurgery since then.'

'So I could be a father a second time?' He tried, how he tried, but he couldn't keep the excitement out of his voice.

'A second time—perhaps a third and fourth. It all seems quite likely. I said you'd probably phone the surgeon back.'

'Yes, I will. I certainly will.' He thought for a moment. 'Joy, a few weeks ago, that would have been the best news in the world. Now…well, it's just great.'

'Yes. You're already going to have a child.' Her voice was neither friendly nor angry. Her detachment made him shiver.

'You knew what this would mean to me,' he said. 'The chances are I never would have seen that article. Why did you show it to me, why did you phone that surgeon?'

Her voice was still flat. 'You now know that possibly—probably—you can father more children. You don't need me. There's no need to enter into a…marriage of convenience so you can be the father of my child.'

'Joy, that's unfair! You know I loved you well before you got pregnant!'

'Yes, I did. Well, I think I did. But each time we got near to talking about our future, you backed away. The first time we…when my baby was conceived you had already said you wouldn't marry me.'

'I said I couldn't marry you,' he corrected. 'Joy, I didn't offer you marriage because I thought you deserved the chance to have children. You were born to be a mother. I couldn't take that from you, no matter how much I loved you.'

'Perhaps,' she said, 'perhaps. Certainly you were very eager to marry me when you found that I was pregnant. If just once you had asked me before it happened…but you didn't. Chris, now I'm not the only chance you have of being a father, can you honestly say that you'd want to marry me if I wasn't pregnant?'

'Yes! I love you, I've loved you since I first saw you, I want to marry you—tomorrow if we can get a licence.'

'We can't,' she said practically. 'Now, answer me another question. Does me being pregnant make you even more eager to marry me?'

It was a fair question but it was also a trick one. He could lie, of course, but that wasn't in his nature. Slowly he said, 'I would have thought that nothing could have made me want to marry you even more. But your having a baby did.'

'I'm glad you're honest with me,' she said. 'Chris, I don't know what's to become of us. You've turned my life upside down. I think I still need time to work out what I really want, whether I can really trust you.'

He seized on this small opening. 'You're back at

work,' he said, 'we're talking to each other. Let's carry on like this, there's no need for any sudden decisions.'

'All right. Now I've come back to work but you can at least welcome me back with a hug.'

So he hugged her. One of his arms was round her neck, the other clutched her waist. And as he pulled her to him he could feel the thickening of her figure, the bulge where previously there had been none. It was magic!

Joy knew what he was doing. After an all too short time she gently pushed him away. 'You're supposed to be hugging me,' she pointed out with a wry smile, 'not deciding if my baby's doing all right.'

'Can't I do both?'

'Evidently. But I am here to work. My doctor thinks it would be a good thing if I put in a few weeks before I started maternity leave proper.'

'Your doctor said that?'

'Not my GP, your good friend David Garner. Of course, I wouldn't dream of thinking that he said it so that we would be thrown together again. His decision was a purely medical one.'

'Of course it was. But I think I'll still buy him a bottle of single malt on my way home tonight.'

'Good.' Suddenly she was brisk. 'Now, that's enough talking. I called in and the shift leader says they're busy again. Do you want to carry on here, and I'll go and help out in the delivery suite?'

'No. You coming here has disturbed me. I need to do something. I'll go and deliver babies.' He pointed to the intray, full of papers. 'That lot came this morning. Want to deal with it?'

She groaned. 'I feel ill again. I'd forgotten every morning's paperchase. You go, I'll make a start on it.

Before he went he kissed her gently on the lips. 'I love you,' he said.

'You mean you love us both,' she corrected, but it was said with a half-smile.

The delivery suite *was* busy, so busy, in fact, that the shift leader had no time to gossip about Joy's return.

'There's Della Drake, a primigravida, just come into room 3. Brought herself in in a taxi. There's a student midwife with her now, but it would help if you could see to her, Chris.'

'I'm on my way.'

He still had time to run over Della Drake's notes. She was 37, one of the many slightly older mums they were seeing now. At present she was in stage one.

He pushed open the door. 'Hello, Mrs Drake—mind if I call you Della? My name's Chris McAlpine. I'm your midwife.'

He noted the ring on the anxious woman's finger. 'You married, Della? Has your husband been told you've come in here?'

'I left a message for him. He's out, looking for a job. Chris, Ken's a...nervous sort of man.'

Chris picked up the overtones when Della used the word 'nervous'. He knew he would have to look out for Ken, when and if he eventually got there. But that wasn't an immediate problem. He smiled again and said, 'We'll try to make him feel at home. Now, if I could just take a few readings, Della. We'll start with your blood pressure.'

A couple of hours later he heard the sound of raised voices outside, and then the door was banged open. The man framed there was large, red-faced, once muscular but now slightly fat. Chris heard Della wail from behind him, 'Ken!'

'Who're you?' the man asked belligerently.

Chris was sitting, filling in the usual forms. He decided to remain sitting, he was less of a threat that way. 'I'm Chris McAlpine, the midwife in charge of your wife. It's Ken, isn't it? You'll be pleased to know that your wife and baby are both doing well. If you'd like to come here and—'

'I don't want a man messing with my wife!'

'Ken! Chris has been very good. He—'

'It's Chris, is it, now?'

'Mr Drake!' Chris knew he had to calm the situation. 'The last thing your wife needs is this kind of noise, this kind of behaviour. Now, if you'd just like to—'

'I said I didn't want you messing with my wife!'

Now Chris stood. When he walked over to the man he could smell his breath—there was alcohol there certainly. The man was dangerously excited. Perhaps he should inform security.

But from behind him there came a sudden gasp. His patient was in pain. He turned, moved over to her. 'I think…something's happening,' Della panted. 'I felt something move and—'

'I'll get you some gas and air if you like,' Chris said as he gently examined her. 'That'll make you feel better and—'

'Don't you turn your back on me!'

Chris ignored the angry voice behind him and finished his examination. He fitted the Entonox mask over Della's nose and mouth, waited till she had taken a couple deep breaths and saw the tenseness disappear as the painkiller started to work. Then he turned to face the woman's husband.

Ken had picked up a chair and was holding it over his head.

Chris clasped his hands behind him, tried to look as unthreatening as possible. 'Ken, your wife's having her first child. She's excited, just like you. You both need to keep calm. D'you know, she was worried about you? Worried about how you'd feel? I think that's pretty amazing, being able to think about you and your troubles when she's in so much pain herself. I think she's quite a woman. You're a lucky man.'

'She's all right is Della,' Ken said cautiously.

'She's more than all right.' Chris moved to one side. 'Look at her, Ken, come and hold her hand. She needs you, she needs to know you love her.'

Ken lowered the chair, but kept hold of it. 'What d'you know about what she needs?'

'Like I said, you're a lucky man, Ken. I had the chance of a wonderful woman myself but I lost her. Don't you do the same. In an hour or two you'll have a child, in a couple of days you'll have a wife and a newborn baby at home. They're going to need all the help, all the support you can give them. And they'll both love you in return. That's quite something.'

'Are you an expert or what?'

Chris shrugged. 'I'm not married, Ken. But put it this way, if I could change places with you now, I'd do it like a shot. A loving wife, that's really something. A loving wife and a child to look after. That's something more. You don't want to spoil it all, do you? Now, let go of that chair and come and hold your wife's hand.'

There was silence in the room, and then Ken did as he was told. Outwardly, Chris remained as calm as ever. Inwardly, he breathed a sigh of relief. The problem was over. Somehow he knew there'd be no more trouble.

'Have you got a moment Midwife McAlpine?'

He blinked and turned. There, just inside the door,

was Joy. He hadn't heard her come in, had no idea how long she'd been watching.

'I think everything's all right here for a minute,' he said, and followed her out of the door.

'I heard what you said to that man,' she said when they were in the corridor. 'You kept on repeating the same thing over and over—love. It hypnotised him. But you meant every word of it, didn't you?'

'I didn't know you were listening,' he said, 'but, yes, I meant every word I said.'

'You told him you'd had a wonderful woman but you'd lost her. Did you mean me?'

'Of course. You're the only woman in my life.'

'Hmm. Well, you'd better get back to your patient, hadn't you?' Joy's voice suddenly softened. 'When she's had the baby, come and see me.'

There was no more trouble from Ken. Three hours later he became the father of a large baby girl and excitedly told Chris that she'd be called Donna. 'Donna and Della, y'know…sound great together, don't they?'

'I think they sound good,' Chris agreed, 'but check what your wife thinks.' Della squeezed his hand. 'Thank you for everything,' she whispered, 'and I don't just mean helping me have the baby.'

'Don't think about it. Ken'll be a fine father.' Then mother, baby and father went out towards the postnatal ward and Chris crossed off Della's name from the whiteboard in the midwives' station. His job with her was done.

As requested, he went round to see Joy in her—their—office. 'Are you doing anything special tonight?' she asked him.

'Nothing really special. Go home and cook tea.'

'In that case, can I come home and have tea with you?'

It was later that evening. Once again James and Anna had gone out together, announcing that they might be very late back. 'In fact,' James had said, 'I might stay over at Anna's for the night. There's a spare bed there.'

'I'm sure there is,' Chris had replied, wondering if it was going to be used.

'That couple had a distinctly self-satisfied air,' Joy had said, 'as if something they had been planning had worked out.'

'Don't know what you're talking about,' Chris had answered. 'Certainly nothing to do with me.'

Joy had come back to his house for tea, and now they lay side by side in his bed. Chris couldn't resist touching, stroking her naked body. They had made sweet, gentle love and she lay there drowsily, eyes half-closed, content with what he was doing.

He caressed her breasts, slightly heavier than before, the nipples darkened by pregnancy. The curve of her belly was obvious, the skin almost translucent, with the blue of veins here and there. He kissed the warmth of them.

'Things are going to be all right,' she told him. 'We've got over one hurdle, we've got each other, there's no need to make plans. Soon we can, but not yet.'

'But I want to talk about names,' he protested. 'How about Anna if it's a girl and James if it's a boy?'

'Chris McAlpine! You're an old sentimentalist.' Joy paused. 'But it's still an interesting idea.'

Then they were silent for a while, silent and content. 'There is something we ought to think about,' Chris said. 'If I have this operation, and if everything goes well, how many more children should we have?'

Joy giggled. 'Wait till I've had one. You've heard mums in labour swearing blind that after this one they'll never have another.'

'I've heard them,' he said. 'The funny thing is, they always change their minds. Now, the next thing. When do we announce that I'm the father of bump here?'

Joy frowned. 'Look, Christmas is coming up, there's going to be enough excitement. I think we should wait till afterwards. If that's all right with you?'

'The sooner the better for me. But we'll do what you say. Though I have some ideas of my own about a pram.'

'I might have guessed that. Incidentally, what are we going to do about Christmas Day?'

'I'll cook you Christmas dinner,' he said promptly. 'Dinner for you and Anna.'

'What a lovely idea! All right, I accept—if Ma agrees, that is. And then you can be my guest at the hospital New Year ball.'

'The Hogmanay Ball?' Chris asked. 'I've heard of it, it's supposed to be a really swish social occasion.'

'It is. We have a surprising number of Scotsmen in the hospital. Well, a surprising number of men who think they're entitled to wear a kilt.'

'I like a bit of show,' he said, and thought for a minute. 'Incidentally, what colour dress will you wear?'

'That's an odd question.' Joy looked surprised. 'Obviously something that's not too tight-waisted, something that goes with bump here. I've got a black one in mind.'

'Black is fine,' he said, and kissed her.

EPILOGUE

NEW Year's Eve. Chris had intended to pick Joy up and drive to the Cliff Hotel, where the ball was to be held, in style. But he was working during the day, and at the end of his shift there were just not enough midwives to go round.

'I can work another couple of hours,' he told the shift leader. 'I've got what I'm wearing tonight with me.'

'Chris, you're a darling. There's not a lot of people would do this for me on New Year's Eve.'

Then he phoned Joy and told her what was happening. It was Joy's unit—she could understand and sympathise. 'I'll get Ma to run me to the hotel and meet you there. The foyer at half past eight?'

'I'll be there. Love you, sweetheart.'

James and Anna were having a quiet evening in together, having already agreed to pick Joy and Chris up at the end of the ball. Chris was looking forward to the occasion.

In fact, things worked out easier than he had thought. He was attending a primigravida, expecting the usual long-drawn-out first delivery. But Freda O'Toole was one of those rare women for whom giving birth was no more trouble than any other slightly physical exertion. She didn't want gas and air, she apparently felt no pain, just a little discomfort, she chattered non-stop through the delivery and was absolutely delighted with her little girl.

'All these stories I've heard about how terrible it

was,' she said cheerfully. 'All nonsense. Now I've had one I'm going to have another four.'

'It's not always like this,' Chris said cautiously. 'It can be more complicated.'

'Well, you've been a lovely man to me, and I hope I have a male midwife next time. You're going to the party now? Chris, if you have a minute, will you come down to the ward and let me see you in your finery? I'd really like that.'

'Most new mums just want to sleep,' he said. 'But if you want I'll call in.'

Quickly he showered, then turned to the case where he'd brought what he was to wear. It felt odd at first— but then he felt at home again. Feeling slightly foolish, he went along to the postnatal ward and asked if he could see Freda O'Toole. A slightly goggle-eyed staff nurse let him in, an equally goggle-eyed Freda couldn't believe that he was the white-suited man who had helped her deliver the baby.

'They say clothes make the man,' she gasped. 'What a man they've made you.'

'I'm just a male midwife,' he told her.

Fortunately he had no trouble getting a taxi to the hotel as it was still early in the evening. He arrived a quarter of an hour before he was to meet Joy, and went into the men's cloakroom to check his dress. Joy had been right, everyone did make an effort tonight. There were more than a few kilted Scotsmen, and the rest were in the traditional evening dress. And there was him.

It was time. He went through to the foyer. He nodded to a couple of people he knew, smiled and talked to a couple more. And then he saw Joy.

She was a vision. He didn't know what she had done to her hair, but it had been highlighted and flowed in mass of curls to her shoulders. Her dress was black, some darkly shining material, with a cleverly cut loose top that disguised the fact that she was pregnant. Her skirt was long but tight and slashed to midthigh. He could see other people staring at her admiringly.

When he walked towards her she blinked. He leaned forward, kissed her on the cheek. 'You look ravishing,' he said.

'*I* look ravishing! Aren't you the fancy one?'

'My regimental mess dress,' he said, wondering if perhaps he'd made a mistake. 'I'm in the Reserves, I'm entitled to wear it. Anyway, remember peacocks are male.'

'Chris, you look wonderful. And when people look at us dancing, I'll wonder if they're looking at me or you.'

He was wearing dark blue trousers with a scarlet flash down the side, a short scarlet jacket with gold on the shoulders and cuffs. As he'd said, it was his regimental mess dress. 'Nearly two hundred years ago the officers in my regiment sat down dressed like this on the night before Waterloo,' he said. 'The night after, half of them were missing. It's a uniform I'm proud to wear.'

'And I'm proud to be seen with a man who's wearing it. Come on, I want to show you off.'

It was to be a formal dance so they joined the receiving line and their names were announced loudly by the master of ceremonies. 'Miss Joy Taylor and Major Christopher McAlpine, MC.'

'MC?' she whispered.

'Short for MCP. Which is short for Male Chauvinist Pig.'

She pinched his arm viciously. 'Tell me! I want to know.'

'It's the Military Cross. As with all medals, it means I was lucky but I guess I am proud to wear it.'

'I'll bet you were lucky… Oh, Chris look! Another uniform just like yours!'

'David Garner. You know we were in the same regiment, we plotted this together. Come over and meet Mary, his wife, she's lovely.'

Joy knew she was going to enjoy herself. She had the feeling that this was more than the end of a year, it was the beginning of a new year, and for her a new life. She had seen—been secretly pleased with—the astonished looks people had given them when they'd seen her with Chris. There would be no hiding who her baby's father was now.

David and Mary were delighted to see them and they looked for a table together. 'Now I can ask,' Mary said. 'Would the pair of you like to come to dinner quite soon?'

'We'd love to,' said Joy.

After that, they danced. It didn't surprise her at all that Chris was a good dancer. And he could lead her. She hadn't been to a dance for months, she thought she'd be clumsy, have forgotten everything. But as he whirled her round, she felt she had the skills of a ballerina. 'I love dancing with you,' she said.

'I love just being with you.'

For some reason their table was intensely popular. Joy's male friends came over and asked her to dance. They would chat a while, then ask airily, 'Nice chap, Chris McAlpine. See a lot of him?'

'Well, he's in my unit. Of course I see a lot of him. Good of him to ask me here, wasn't it?'

'Apart from you, every man I've danced with has wanted to know if you're the father of my baby,' she whispered to Chris when they had a minute together. 'But none of them has dared ask me directly.'

'The minute you've been on the floor, I've been approached by ladies who've asked me to dance. I mean, it's quite proper, we midwives have to hang together, it's not as if I'm a real man. And each one of them has asked outright—am I the father of your child?'

Joy giggled. 'What have you said?'

'I just look serious and say it's for the mother to announce the name of the father. I wouldn't dream of speaking before her.'

'Very wise. Have you noticed I've avoided going to the ladies'? I know the minute I get in there, there'll be a stream of friends after me demanding details, and I haven't decided what to say yet.'

'You'll have to decide soon. Come on, it'll soon be midnight. We all have to be dancing to greet the new year. What d'you think of the master of ceremonies?'

'He's good, isn't he? You know he's our head of Security, he does this every year. He loves it.'

'He's been beaming at us all evening,' said Chris. Now, just say the word, and I'll go and stop him.'

'Stop him what? Stop him smiling?'

Chris swung her expertly out of the way of a heavyweight couple who'd perhaps had too much to drink. 'Wouldn't dream of doing that. No, I suppose I could stop him announcing our engagement.'

'Our what? Chris McAlpine, what have you done?'

'Well, you know I love you and I know we'll be happy. All three of us.'

'Three of us?'

'Well, three to start with. Look, you don't really want me to stop him saying that we want to get married, do you? He's obviously looking forward to it.'

'But, Chris, I—'

'Ladies and gentlemen. In two minutes we'll start the countdown to New Year. But before we do that…I have a very happy task to perform. Joy Taylor has been with us for…'

Chris leaned over and kissed her. 'Too late now,' he said.

Modern Romance™
...seduction and
passion guaranteed

Tender Romance™
...love affairs that
last a lifetime

Sensual Romance™
...sassy, sexy and
seductive

Blaze
...sultry days and
steamy nights

Medical Romance™
...medical drama on
the pulse

Historical Romance™
...rich, vivid and
passionate

29 new titles every month.

*With all kinds of Romance for
every kind of mood...*

MILLS & BOON®

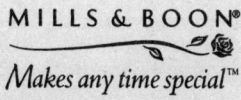

Makes any time special™

MAT4

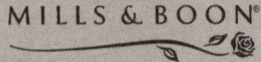

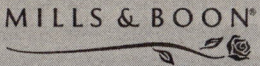

MILLS & BOON®

Christmas
with a Latin Lover

Three brand-new stories

Lynne Graham

Penny Jordan

Lucy Gordon

Published 19th October

4 FREE

books and a surprise gift!

We would like to take this opportunity to thank you for reading th
Mills & Boon® book by offering you the chance to take FOU
more specially selected titles from the Medical Romance™ seri
absolutely FREE! We're also making this offer to introduce you
the benefits of the Reader Service™—

- ★ FREE home delivery
- ★ FREE gifts and competitions
- ★ FREE monthly Newsletter
- ★ Exclusive Reader Service discounts
- ★ Books available before they're in the shops

Accepting these FREE books and gift places you under
obligation to buy, you may cancel at any time, even after receivi
your free shipment. Simply complete your details below and retu
the entire page to the address below. *You don't even need a stamp*

YES! Please send me 4 free Medical Romance books and a surpr
gift. I understand that unless you hear from me, I will recei
6 superb new titles every month for just £2.49 each, postage a
packing free. I am under no obligation to purchase any books a
may cancel my subscription at any time. The free books and gift v
be mine to keep in any case.

M1Z

Ms/Mrs/Miss/Mr ....Initials.................................
                                                                BLOCK CAPITALS PLEA

Surname ....

Address ....

....

....Postcode...................................

Send this whole page to to:
UK: FREEPOST CN81, Croydon, CR9 3WZ
EIRE: PO Box 4546, Kilcock, County Kildare (stamp required)